WHAT HAPPENED WAS IMPOSSIBLE

E. F. SCHRAEDER

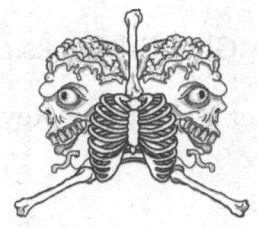

Ghoulish Books
an imprint of Perpetual Motion Machine Publishing
San Antonio, Texas

What Happened Was Impossible
Copyright © 2023 E. F. Schraeder

All Rights Reserved

ISBN: 978-1-943720-85-9

The story included in this publication is a work of fiction. Names, characters, places and incidents are products of the author's imagination or are used fictitiously. Any resemblance to actual events or locales or persons living or dead is entirely coincidental.

Without limiting the rights under copyright reserved above, no part of this publication may be reproduced, stored in or introduced into a retrieval system, or transmitted, in any form, or by any means (electronic, mechanical, photocopying, recording, or otherwise), without the prior written permission of both the copyright owner and the above publisher of this book.

www.GhoulishBooks.com

Cover by Matthew Revert

"We are each our own devil, and we make this world our hell."

—Oscar Wilde

"The final forming of a person's character lies in their own hands."

—Anne Frank

"We are each our own devil, and we make this world our hell."

—Oscar Wilde

TABLE OF CONTENTS

I.

A SAD CHILDHOOD

HOW SHE DIED

Fay Parker, Medical Examiner

A LOT OF stories like this start with the body of a woman. This time, the body belonged to a mother. That made it different than the usual dead women I stare at. I knew this one's name and address before taking a look at her.

She was no schoolgirl nabbed by a dangerous, psychopathic stranger or handsy neighbor. She wasn't an anonymous college woman who stayed out late partying too hard with the wrong friends or taking risks on the streets. She wasn't an offbeat loner roaming the edge of town at night looking for drugs or other sorts of trouble that happens. Murder was never anyone's debt for poor choices.

No. But this body belonged to a woman who'd followed the rules. Made safe choices. Lived up to expectations. At least until the point where she separated from her husband. He'd be a suspect, of course, but still. Staring at it for the first time. This body pushed against the script, and therefore threatened to make less sense. Yet somehow, this body ended up just as dead.

Caroline Wright. Fifty-four. About five foot six inches tall, Caroline was a white woman with a medium build and long, light auburn hair twisted into a tidy bun. A smear of crimson lipstick on her parted lips. Caroline was ultimately, quintessentially average. A middle-class white woman living on a cul-de-sac like a hundred other houses in a colorless suburban street. Hers was the kind of development that came out of redlined districts back in the day, surrounded by comparable houses each of which looked a little outdated. This body belonged inside one of those houses doing dishes or making dinner, not twisted in a sticky swirl of blood and sour puddle of urine.

Until this morning, Caroline's body was that of a comfortable wife and mother of two teenagers: one boy and one girl, Ida and Jade. Two average kids who, from the awards lining the hallway, I suspected got decent grades. Also from the photos I figured there were very few distinguishing interests or features about them other than matching waves of strawberry blond hair. Two bland kids with bland lives, few extracurricular activities, and perhaps even fewer problems. Until now. Starting tomorrow, their lives would be permanently scarred by this scene.

The only curiosity about her children was how two well-off kids could manage to be so completely uninteresting and uninspiring. The mother who produced those kids seemed like part of some kind of abstracted, imaginary U.S. average. That of a good life.

That body wasn't supposed to be so miserable she'd slice open her own throat.

But that's exactly what appeared to have happened with Caroline Wright. On the day she died, Caroline was alone in her bathroom. She must have suffered at the time of death. According to her children, husband, co-workers, and neighbors, and everyone the cops spoke to, no one in her life could have predicted, imagined, or remotely suspected she was on the verge of committing the ultimate irreversible act. Suicide wasn't something she spoke of.

But that's what I was probably going to declare it. Suicide. Though it seemed improbable, Caroline's suicide was not impossible.

What I knew was this: Caroline left no note at the scene. But there was also a lack of struggle, no defensive wounds to suggest she'd fought anyone or tried to protect herself. The house showed no signs of forced entry. In fact, there was a complete lack of evidence of any kind. Nothing indicating an intruder or even a guest had entered the house on the morning of the incident. All the fingerprints belonged to family members. And all of those family members provided completely verifiable alibis during Caroline's estimated time of death.

Suicide. Because there were no signs of an intruder and because nothing was missing. Without an attempted burglary, there was no reason to suspect any wrongdoing or robbery gone wrong.

Suicide. Because the husband was where he claimed to be and the kids were at school.

Suicide. Because Caroline had no rivals at work, no hidden romances, no conflicts with neighbors or anyone in her life. Everyone spoke about her with a restrained disinterest. Restrained because it seemed rude not to care about her now that she was dead.

Suicide. Because there were no other options.

Just the same, the death and the scene of the event seemed unusual. Self-stabbing wasn't exactly a popular way for middle-aged women to kill themselves. Poisoning was the common choice. Statistically. Not women like Caroline who were settled into the grooves of their lives. Not women who were dressed like they were going on a mid-day luncheon date with friends. Not women who had played all the odds and found comfort. It was girls who were at risk of suicide because by the odds, among the female of the species, it was teenaged girls who were most likely to die by suicide. Probably because girls were so fucking impulsive.

In most countries, suicide was more successful— meaning more *effective*—for men. Sure, women made almost double the attempts to off themselves, but the common assumption among us medical professionals was that those were manipulative gestures that sometimes landed them in hospitals. The point was, women usually failed at it.

Men knew how to do that shit. Men died more than twice as often as women by suicide. Men made capable, fast, irreversible decisions. Also because men made solid choices when it came time to pick a lethal method.

Not so for this woman. Caroline lived up to her name. Caroline Wright did suicide right.

A spatter of blood coated the tiled walls. Red dripped from the mirror, and pooled on the floor by Caroline Wright's head. But that wasn't the ugliest image at the scene.

The slipped-open flesh of her neck left a gaping wound, with a small lesion exposing her trachea. On inspection, the wound displayed hesitation marks. That meant she'd paused at some point, then pressed deeper, cutting in and pulling up. She jammed the blade along her throat, and the slice lines showed every moment of her decision.

From the polished appearance to the attire, this didn't look like the typical image of someone in a state of despair. Prone in a pool of her own blood, though she was wearing a fancy black dress and a good pair of heels, like she intended to go out. But that wasn't the worst part, either.

Although the agony in her contorted mouth suggested tremendous pain, and the twisted position of her arms indicated a degree of uncontrolled convulsions or twitching, the worst part wasn't the expression even as she lay there bleeding, face up, her mouth curled in terror. The worst part wasn't that one wedge-heeled black shoe, half off her foot. A recent pedicure obvious from the deep shiny red polish on her toenails. Not even those half open eyelids, drooped with a mist of silver-green eyeshadow bothered me. The worst part wasn't even the fly that landed on the pinch of rouge smudging her motionless cheek.

The worse part was the fucking bathmat. Specifically, the way the blood sank below the fuzzy sky-blue thing, sticking to the rubberized backing. The thick fibers curdling with organic matter, drenched as it soaked up her blood and piss. Right in front of the basin sink. The bathmat, no one could doubt, had been carefully selected to match the hint of flecked color in the subway tile around the soaker tub. Every element of the newly update room—other than the corpse—was a testament to expensive taste. This was a goddamned nice bathroom. The bathmat had been meant as a finishing touch. *Her finishing touch.*

The worst part was knowing Caroline had picked that thing up at a store and paid a nice penny for it before she bled to death all over it.

***

Fay covered her mouth and nose then leaned over the body. "Best guess? Airway compromise and catastrophic hemorrhage." She took a step back. "I'll know more after a full workup. Could be self-inflicted, but that's not exactly an easy way to go." She walked to the medicine cabinet, opened it. "No antidepressants in here, but there are a few prescriptions that could do some real damage. There are more common ways for women to kill themselves than slicing their own throats. I'll tell you that." She glanced at the others in the room.

For a moment, no one said a word.

"You're the medical examiner, but I gotta say, it's hard to imagine someone standing in a mirror and staring at themselves while they—" Officer Murdock made a throat slice with a finger across his neck. He scowled, his face pinching into wrinkles. "I hate to say it, but you almost expect something like this to be foul play."

"Like I said, there are easier ways to go if you have your heart set on suicide." Fay folded her arms across her chest.

"Dr. Parker—" Melanie, the newly-promoted detective partnering with Murdock, whispered.

"Call me Fay. Please."

"Fay. Will you do an analysis for possible drugs?" Melanie motioned for a crew to come get the body.

Fay folded her arms across her chest and sighed. "You're thinking someone might've wanted this to look like a suicide."

WHAT HAPPENED WAS IMPOSSIBLE

"Some world we live in, isn't it?" Murdock said.

"You talking to the family?" Fay glanced at her phone as it chimed.

"Duty calls?" Murdock asked.

Fay packed up her notes and headed to the door. "There's no end to death."

FATHER OF THE YEAR

Robert Wright, husband of the deceased

I DON'T THINK I can clean that up." Robert Wright staggered out of the bathroom. "But the kids will be coming home from school soon." Robert stood in the second-story hallway of their home shivering. Dark circles patched the skin beneath his blue eyes and his expression was one of exhausted strain. "I don't want my kids to see what—"

"Sir, you should wait downstairs." An unknown voice.

Robert didn't look up. Instead he staggered to the bathroom, his eyes tracing the swirling red patterns on the walls. Anywhere but down.

"Someone will take all of you to headquarters. We're going to be a while."

"Okay," Robert said. He stumbled at the top step, caught himself with one hand on the wall. He didn't recognize anyone moving inside his home. It was too full of people, of their cluttering movements and the business of body removal. No one but the unknown officer spoke to him. He struggled to remember how they all came to be inside. The officers must've introduced themselves, but he couldn't recall. Robert trudged down the steps and made his way to the living room, fell onto the familiar corner of the blue couch.

WHAT HAPPENED WAS IMPOSSIBLE

None of this is real. This can't be real. I don't believe this is happening.

That's what the blank expression in Robert's eyes said. Until he looked down.

Five minutes or more must've passed by the time he noticed his hands. Something like a shrieking wail erupted from some hidden, childlike part of himself when he realized what the red stains were covering his palms and spotting his clothes. The house smelled of death.

A middle-aged woman with a light brown complexion sat across the room. She was dressed in business casual khakis and a loose-fitting beige sweater like someone on a mission to be as unobtrusive as possible.

"Mr. Wright. Mr. Wright, can you hear me?"

Robert twitched once as a scream caught in his throat, thick like a cough. His whole body convulsed like he'd been subjected to a bolt of electricity. Then he looked up. Nodded without blinking, without moving another muscle.

"Sir, my name is Angela Martinez. We need to arrange someone to pick up the children at school so they don't see—this." She bit her lower lip, forcing a pause. "Mr. Wright?"

Robert said nothing. He didn't give any indication he heard a word of it. He swayed side to side like a child attempting to self-soothe. Unsuccessfully.

"Do you understand me?" Ms. Martinez pulled a manilla file folder from her bag and jotted something down. She tilted her head toward Robert. "Mr. Wright, can you hear me?"

Robert straightened upright. He nodded once, but barely.

"Can you tell me where your children, where Ida and Jade, go to school?"

She glanced at a sheet of paper fastened to a clipboard on her lap. Her pen hovered over it like she was taking an inventory.

Yes, that's exactly what she's doing. Ms. Martinez is taking an inventory of my behavior. Responsiveness. Snap out of it.

"High school. Our kids both go to Madison. Their mom took them this morning."

Tears poured from his eyes then as the dots began to connect about the hum of what was happening all around them. He wiped his hands on his pants, smearing the red from his palms.

A gurney carried by two men crated out something covered with a smooth plastic sheet. A hushed murmur of voices spilled down the steps. Bile rose in the back of his throat.

Robert's life blinked in and out of possible explanations like lights turning on and off in his head. He brought his attention to the woman across from him, struggling to concentrate. *Angela. Ms. Martinez. My children. They can't go upstairs.* He sat up straight.

Robert closed his hand over his mouth, swallowed a wave of nausea. "Yes. Please. If someone could get them. Where will they—?" He broke off. His head dropped and he sobbed without stopping. "They can't step into this house. Not now." *Not into this nightmare.*

But it wasn't a nightmare. This was his life now.

THE AFTERMATH

Ida Wright, son of the deceased

"NO, I DIDN'T ask where he was going. It's not like he lives with us now. I thought he was at work like always."

Ida stared at his hands folded on the table.

"Is there a reason you're talking to us separately?" He glanced up at the officer sitting across from him, then answered his own question. "Sorry. I know, I know. You ask the questions." He shrugged. "We're probably all suspects or something now, right?"

Ida brought both hands to his lap, sucked in a deep breath. He rubbed a small spot on his jeans with a thumb. Then Ida froze still like he'd been suddenly stunned. He was barely moving. His blue eyes like pale moons as he blinked, but he didn't cry. He couldn't.

"You're probably in shock." Melanie shifted in her chair. "Do you need anything?"

Murdock moved to the back of the room. "Sometimes for young people, it's hard to express emotions. It's okay."

Ida nodded. "Thanks. Nothing is coming out the way you'd expect. I probably seem pretty confused."

"We understand. Take your time." Melanie leaned forward.

After that, Ida answered the questions one at a time until eventually his voice got quieter.

"I'm sorry. I guess I'm getting really tired." Ida spoke to the tall policeman, still standing in the back of the room. "This is kind of overwhelming."

"You need a break?" The cop in the back of the room ran a brown hand along the stubble on his chin.

Ida shook his head, a fold of stringy hair flopped over one eye. "No thanks, I'm okay. I want to help. Help you find out what happened, I mean."

"We won't be much longer." Melanie rapped the table with one hand then brought them together like she was praying.

***

By the time Ida and what remained of his family left the station, the whole town knew. A dead mother and a father under suspicion. That kind of news was almost too much for a close-knit community town to handle.

The family sedan had been followed all the way from the police station, but Robert didn't say anything until he turned the corner toward home and saw the lawn of their split-level home peppered with people. "Vultures." Ida's dad shook his head. "I know I don't have to remind you, but please don't say anything to anyone about what's happening—okay, kids?"

The serene cul-de-sac had been an ideal place for families. Until the bloodstains splattered the bathroom walls. A few people were snapping pictures of their house.

Jade rolled her eyes. "Come on, Dad. They're just doing their jobs." She glared at him.

Robert opened his mouth to reply, but stopped himself.

WHAT HAPPENED WAS IMPOSSIBLE

"Who, journalists? Bloggers? Pssh! What about privacy? This is a tragedy we're dealing with. Our tragedy." Ida's face reddened, but he still didn't cry.

"Thanks, son."

"We won't say anything." Ida smiled at his dad in the rearview mirror and pressed a foot into the back of his sister's seat.

"Suck up." Jade reached behind her and swatted Ida's leg.

"Good boy," Robert said.

DEAD ENDS

BEFORE IDA'S MOM died, no one thought twice about her. She was cheery and sweet, almost as invisible as a superhero. When the police came to collect a few of her things, Robert protested.

"Those are her things. Her diaries. What do you think they're looking for?" Robert asked. His pale complexion started to flush.

Robert's attorney, Jason Jules, set a hand on his shoulder. "Easy, Robert. Anything she wrote about could be a clue. You never know what's going to be relevant in a case like this. Take a seat. This is good."

A scowl tugged the corners of Robert's mouth down, but he sat at the kitchen table. Jason pulled out a chair and sat beside him.

"I barely feel like I belong here."

Jason set a light brown hand on Robert's pale one, tapping. "Sit still. You're on the mortgage and you two never even bothered to file for separation. It's better for your kids now if you just come home."

"I can't pretend like any of this is normal." Robert pointed to the police hauling out boxes. He brushed something from his eyes and shook his head.

"This means they're investigating, Robert. It's good for you. It'll be done soon."

Robert relaxed. "We were happy. I can't imagine who would've done this to her."

Jason nodded, a slight grin on his face.

***

Back at the station, Detective Warren Murdock pored over Caroline Wright's journals. Sitting at his desk, flipping through them, he hoped for a hint of clarity. Any bit of evidence that Caroline had suffered some kind of catastrophic emotional event or recorded a possible threat. Something that had been unknown to her family and friends. He shoved the journal aside.

"Caroline's journals are a bust. This lady was basically keeping track of her own schedule in here. Nothing. It's little more than a day planner."

"No confessions, then? No affairs? Angry teacher meetings, or problems with the PTA?" Melanie slid into a chair at the desk across from Murdock.

"Not a fucking thing, Mel."

"How far back did you go?"

"Far enough. She loved her kids, liked her job. She thought her marriage would work out." Warren pushed several journals onto the corner of his desk then stacked them into a box. "I'll probably give them back to the husband by the end of the week. After we hear from Fay and close this out as a suicide, I mean. This lady was a real apple pie type."

"I thought it'd be the husband." She slugged back some coffee and made a sour face.

"Everyone did." Murdock shrugged. "It usually is. I gotta say, though . . . if anyone else in the family was a suspect, it'd be the daughter."

"The daughter?" Melanie's eyes opened wide. "Jade?"

"Believe it or not. She's the one Caroline had the

most tension with." Murdock picked up a journal and flipped it open.

He cleared his throat like he was preparing for a speech. "It's not much, but listen to this. 'Jade's a funny kid. She doesn't spend as much time at home as she did last year. She's gotten detached, almost isolated. Hardly talks to me anymore, and snaps when she does. Her new band practice schedule keeps her late after school, but still. I can't shake the feeling she's hiding something. To be so withdrawn and angry at her age, when the whole world should be opening up to her. Maybe it's hormones. God, I hope that's all it is.' And then a note below that with a little heart. She wrote, 'Ida is still my same sweet boy.' Nothing about the husband." He shrugged.

"I thought all teens were a pain in the ass?" Melanie flipped through another journal.

"You'd think. But if anything's strange about that young man, and believe me I thought there was plenty strange about him, it's that his mother adored him so much."

TWO MONTHS LATER

Jade Moore, Sister-in-Law of the deceased

AFTER THE SITUATION with his mother, Caroline, I expected the worst. I moved in to help my brother in the short term. Not because he begged me to, but because I wanted to be there for him, for the kids.

I don't know what I was worried about, because if anything Robert's fine. And the kids? Who knows. They're teenagers. They're not okay on a good day, let alone what happened with their mom.

Ida's nothing like his sister Jade. She's taking it hard. I think she resents me being here, and I'm only here to help. But Ida's still a great kid, kind and smart. I've never so much as redirected him, let alone yell at him or punish him. That boy doesn't even return library books late. He's the kind of kid who looks out for young ones. Whether it was teaching them to tie their shoes, helping them cross the street, or volunteering for afterschool tutoring. All he cares about is other people. He's a good boy.

When he said he wanted to work at the pool teaching young kids to swim and lifeguarding, Robert said yes. I cheered him on, too. Jade made fun of him, of course. But getting involved with something seemed like a great step. Helping people could be the thing to get him back on track after losing his mom that way. He was looking ahead. I was happy for him. It was time to stop looking back at that crazy mom who left him, left all of them.

I hoped spending time at the pool, taking on a real job would help him make friends in his class, too. Lifeguards were always popular. Everyone loved them when I was growing up. I pictured the big sunglasses and chlorine-bleached, stiff hair. A dot of sunscreen across his cheeks and nose.

Ida said it wasn't like that anymore.

Ida was an age when most kids were getting into fights or experimenting with sex or drinking or drugs. And instead, he was showing leadership qualities after everything he's been through. So proud of that kid!

He's had some rough times with his sister and at school. What a relief to see the young man he's becoming. He'd be any parent's dream—and that's what I told my brother Robert. Be proud. You've got a good one.

***

One month later

Why'd I encourage Ida about the pool? I don't know anymore. Hindsight!

The pool eats up his free time, and the pay is crap. I wish I could take that enthusiasm back. Just tell him no.

If only I could press rewind. Reset. So many things could be different.

Join a band with your guitar or something, Ida. Go have fun somewhere. Meet a girl or a guy. Go work somewhere else. Anywhere else.

WHAT HAPPENED WAS IMPOSSIBLE

Believe me, when I saw the poster of the third missing kid from our town, my heart sank. I wish I could say it was from compassion, you know? For the poor kid and his family. But it was another boy from the pool. Ida's pool. The missing boy had curly reddish-blonde hair, big blue eyes, a spray of freckles across the nose, and a fair complexion.

The pictures of Ida's childhood were all over the house, and every one of them confirmed it. He looked like Ida, minus eight years or so. They could've been brothers. It made me sick.

Robert said I was being silly, that Ida was practically grown. But still. After losing his mom to that horrible suicide, Ida'd been through enough trauma for two lifetimes. Now he had to hear about a missing boy who could've been his double.

Every time I picked up the paper, I was reminded of it. The missing boy could've easily belonged to Caroline and Robert. That was the truth, and it scared Robert no matter how much he denied it. The vulnerability of his child—I'll never shake the feeling I had when I saw the face, and I'm only Ida's aunt.

How anyone's heart could withstand so much loss I'll never know. Now another family's bad news was spreading, a child's potential splattered across the news.

The panic. The pain. The fear of a loss that would eat you alive. I didn't want to think about what losing Ida would do to Robert. That poor missing boy— Timmy. Oh the likeness just about strangled me. Every article I read online ripped those feelings right to the surface of the skin.

I guess that's selfishness. My knee-jerk wish that I'd insisted Ida take the summer off or that Robert had sent him somewhere else. Somewhere safe, where he could've been far away from all the trouble.

Poor Ida! How the news must feel to him after everything. I only hope he doesn't feel guilty, like he was to blame. Sometimes there's no way to stop people from doing terrible things.

I told him that. The not-to-feel-bad part. He was doing his job and keeping an eye on the swimmers.

No matter how awful it felt, if Timmy left the pool with someone who did this to him, it's not your fault, Ida. That's what I said.

Ida didn't cry, but I could tell he was still worried. Robert's his dad, but I think a woman knows these things, senses them. We pay attention. We can tell.

Robert insisted I was being overly dramatic. Still. I told Ida he didn't have to go back to work, not for the rest of summer. But Ida loved being at the pool, so off he went every day like nothing was wrong. What a trooper!

Since Timmy was probably taken from the place Ida worked, Ida was eventually questioned, along with everyone else from the pool. I hated that he had to go through all that—again. Talking to the police had to trigger some awful memories for him, but he didn't complain.

No one suspected him of any wrongdoing, of course, but they said even a minor detail could crack a case. What I worried about, and what the police seemed to suggest, was that there may be someone profiling kids who looked like Timmy.

I knew what that meant. *Little boys who looked like Ida were in danger*.

My heart broke for all of the lost boys, of course, but I hadn't realized that right away. God, it was true.

WHAT HAPPENED WAS IMPOSSIBLE

All the other kids who vanished were boys. Strawberry blondes. One older than the boy from Ida's pool, but most younger than Timmy.

Two weeks and none of them had been found. Not yet, anyway. It didn't look good for them at this point.

That's about when Ida's night terrors started. Again. That sweet kid didn't even feel safe in his sleep. He couldn't sleep through a single night after talking to the police. Massively triggered a stress reaction, and he's such a sensitive boy. God bless them, they were just doing their jobs, but they scared him half to death.

At breakfast one morning, I decided it was time for him to grow up. Or look like it, anyway. That's what I was trying to convince him of—that he had to be safe. The conversation didn't go well.

***

"I think you should grow a beard," I said.

"What?" Ida frowned.

"I mean it. You'd look good with a little goatee or something. Not a big shaggy thing like so many men wear now. Bring back the manicured look."

"Why?"

One-word answers. That was not like Ida, either. He was really feeling low.

"Well, you'd look older for one thing."

"Oh."

His face paled. A hard thing to imagine on a kid like him. He didn't say anything else while he sat there, noodling around on his phone. Sometimes he was just like everyone else.

"I'd look like Dad."

I laughed before I could stop myself, knowing he would be a dead ringer for his biological father and

Robert. Caroline sure had a type. "You know I'm just thinking about your safety."

Nothing.

"Maybe you should leave the pool. Summer's almost over, anyway."

His face twisted. "Come on, Aunt Jade. I'm not bailing. Those kids would freak out even more."

"You're freaking out."

"No I'm not."

Then his tell. The best thing about having a kid who looked so much like Robert was that I knew red ears meant he was upset and probably lying. I'm not generally suspicious, but I knew that body language. I raised an eyebrow, waiting for clarification.

"So, you're not scared more boys will be kidnapped?"

"Well, geez. Of course it bothers me. I'm not a monster. I worry about them. I'm just not freaking out or anything."

"Uh huh. And you're not disturbed by your resemblance to the boys who've already gone missing?"

He frowned. "Well no. I can't say I like it, but I am way older. I don't think whatever pervert is taking them is going to come after a seventeen-year-old if that's what you're after. God. Stop trying to freak me out."

It wasn't our best chat.

***

The detective stopped by again, asking after Ida. Detectives Melanie Gutierrez and Something Murdock. All mirrored glasses and muscles. They made me uncomfortable, but I decided small talk was a better plan than avoidance.

WHAT HAPPENED WAS IMPOSSIBLE

I gestured, inviting them inside. I told them about my suggestion to Ida. The beard. I asked if they thought something like that may help. I hoped a beard would age him up.

At first they didn't answer. Murdock only shrugged.

"Sometimes these types have a target age, right? Isn't that what the profilers call it?"

He folded his big arms across his chest and nodded. "Something like that, ma'am."

"That's what I thought. Want a coffee?"

"No thanks, ma'am. Do you know when Ida may be back?"

"What's this about? He's already spoken with you."

"We're just crossing our t's and that sort of thing. Following up to get a clearer picture of the day." The woman was petite with bleached blond highlights. Spritely and young.

"Are you talking to all the lifeguards from that day again?"

He nodded. Gutierrez wandered around the room looking at everything. Taking in the whole scene. She looked worried.

Murdock stood up and walked to his partner. "What about Jade? Do you expect her home soon, too?"

A shiver ran through me. *What had she done?* This was closer than I thought.

DREAM TIME

Ida Wright

THE NIGHTMARE WAS always the same. I was coming out of the water and everyone was relieved to şee me. Like I'd been missing or whatever.

I had something in my mouth, pushing into the back of my throat, choking me. It hurt and felt hard, like plastic.

I realized two things simultaneously. I had to get it out. It was a message from someone. Someone bad.

At first I thought it was a note in a baggie. I felt the plastic, stuck no matter how I moved, so I reached in and pull it out. But it wasn't a note. It was a knife.

People around me were taking pictures by then. When they saw the blade they started screaming.

The knife was bigger than it should have been. Like it shouldn't have fit in my mouth at all but there it was. I couldn't explain it. Dreams were weird. But everyone stared and yelled, and I started crying.

How old are you in the dream?

I don't know. A little younger than I am now.

What scares you most about it?

This was a stupid idea. Never mind.

I pressed my palms into my eyes until everything went blurry.

WHAT HAPPENED WAS IMPOSSIBLE

I stopped writing, ripped up the pages, and stuffed them into my pockets. I decided to throw them away at school. I knew my aunt probably read my journals. *Thanks for the privacy.*

The journal became something else for me then.

A friend. An alibi. A comfort. It offered a plea to anyone who read it.

I wrote down a few notes about problem classes. My goals for the future. Shit I knew my nosy aunt would like. Never anything too real because I could be anywhere I imagined inside those pages. No matter what I had planned, I wrote a little bit in it each day. Just like the therapist suggested. In the morning. For evidence. Then I went downstairs for breakfast just like any other day.

***

At school I never needed to hide. Until lately. After what happened with my mom.

I lived in a town too small for tragedies, yet I was surrounded by a lot of them. People started paying attention. Sometimes it was disappointing that my mom's suicide was so good for my popularity. Sometimes, it was awesome.

Now that there were a bunch of missing kids in town, my mom wasn't the main news of the day. It helped a little.

Once the images started circulating of the boys, though. It got worse. The resemblance wasn't something I could avoid. People were talking about it nonstop.

Part of me liked the attention, but mostly I wanted it to go away.

***

"Our son has been missing for two days. The police have told us that with every hour that passes, the risk increases that he won't—" The man on the phone screen stammered, his uncontrollable cries blurted between sentences. *Sloppy.*

Colby laughed. "Wow. Way to keep your composure, dude."

"You're sick. He's a grieving father or whatever, you know?" Lala said.

"He can't be grieving unless he knows the kid's dead. And if he knows the kid's dead, it means he totally did it, so he can't be grieving. He'd be pretending to be grieving. So if he did it, the question is, how well is he pretending to be worried and not grieving? And if he didn't do it, he's just like whatever. I'm upset. My son's gone and everyone thinks I killed him."

"That's sick. You've given that way too much thought, Colby." Lala shook her head, laughing. She blew a wad of gum into a pink bubble until it popped.

Colby shrugged. "I'm into criminology. You've got to think it through. If he seems nervous, it's like, why are you nervous, dude? Two options. One, because we suspect you. Or two, because you did it." He held up his phone and showed the interview again, this time with the sound on mute. "Look at his expression. What do you think he's feeling?"

Lala nodded. "That's messed up that you even thought of doing that."

"Come on. Watch him."

Lala leaned over the screen. "I don't think he seems nervous. He seems sad."

"Thank you! My point exactly. Dude's in the clear." Colby threw his hands up, making the point.

WHAT HAPPENED WAS IMPOSSIBLE

I shoved the lunch tray away. "Oh my God you guys are so stupid. It doesn't matter what he looks like. He's upset. People act all kinds of ways when they're upset. Some people get all zombie-eyed and checked out and shit, some people get really focused and clear, some get emotional. There's not like one way to be a human."

"That is so deep." Lala winked at me. "That you'd even think of that is so smart. That's kind of hot."

This would be one of those moments where the increased attention turned out to be awesome.

Still, I rolled my eyes. Resisting was part of the allure. "Gross. A kid's missing, and all you're doing is obsessing about how to prove yourself." I pointed at Colby. "You're all CSI and shit and totally not thinking about how crap this is for the kid. His family. Wow. Sensitive."

Lala nodded. "Point taken."

"Dude, why so sensitive? Is it cause you're like red-hair-bros or something?" Colby punched me in the arm.

"You know what, man, you're an asshole. I'm out." I left the picnic table and pulled a hat over my head, hiding my reddening ears.

Lala scampered after me. "What's going on? You knew him, didn't you? From the pool?"

"Yeah. I do. Don't use the past tense, okay? He's not dead. Just missing." I tried to ignore her and leaned against a tree, pulling off chunks of bark with one finger.

"Sorry. I guess I wasn't thinking."

"Yeah, there's a lot of that going around." I pushed my thumb to a fingertip, now red and raw from peeling the bark.

"Jesus, I'm trying to say I notice what's going on with you. This can't be easy, especially since . . . But God. You don't have to be such a douchebag."

"Right. I'm the douchebag. Not Captain Asshat over there." I pointed at Colby.

Lala laughed. After a second, I did too.

"It's just upsetting, you know? The cops are asking the lifeguards all these gross questions. My dad is totally ignoring everything, and my aunt's all freaking out." I stuffed both hands into my pockets. Looked away. Lala inched closer to me. This was going very well.

"She probably just wants to know you're safe." Lala touched my forearm, then slid her hand on top of mine. "I do too. After everything with your mom, I mean, this is so soon." She gave my hand a squeeze. "I'm sorry you're dealing with all this again."

She was hooked. Some girls loved tragic cases like me.

I glanced at her. "Nobody's safe. That's just a bullshit illusion people buy into to make themselves feel better."

"Damn. Harsh, Ida."

"Sorry. It's just been a weird morning. Weird year. Weird life. Whatever. I shouldn't have snapped at you." My stupid ears. I felt the pink flush warming, covering my face.

"No worries. You're still my guy, right?" She toyed with the top button of my shirt.

***

"Aunt Jade, you need to back off. You're making me sound like a total creeper."

"Ida! I just told the police they are being unfair asking you to come in again."

WHAT HAPPENED WAS IMPOSSIBLE

I rolled my eyes at her. She's so overprotective. Worse than Mom. I wasn't some stupid kid. "Right. Because harassing white boys is really a thing for cops."

"Geez, Ida. Your generation is so political."

"It's true, Aunt Jade. They're just asking me questions because I was there. They aren't harassing me, and I'm pretty sure that's literally their job. So like, they're allowed to ask. Cool off."

"I just don't want you involved."

Ida shrugged. "I *am* involved. I work there. I was on the clock."

"You don't know anything."

I pulled the hoodie over my head.

"Well, at least eat something before we go." She pointed at a bowl of steaming oatmeal on the counter. "And for Pete's sake don't wear that grungy sweatshirt. You look like a hoodlum."

"Nobody uses that word anymore." Aunt Jade was exhausting.

"Just eat." She nudged the bowl to me.

"Fine." I grabbed a spoon and slid the bowl across the counter.

Jade sipped her coffee. "You're not telling me something."

"Oh my God, Jade! Enough with the ears already. It's not a magic lasso, okay? You can't force me to open up to you just because you feel bad for me after Mom—died."

"You mean golden lasso if you're referring to the great and powerful Wonder Woman, kid. And fine. I'll back off. But I still know you're keeping something from me."

Ida pulled a face. "You know what, I'm nervous. Shocker. Nobody wants to talk to the cops, do they?"

"No, I guess not."

"Thank you."

"Now your whole face is red. You can't go in like that. You look deranged."

I laughed. "Thanks. Great confidence builder, you are. So glad you're staying with us to help."

"And that wild cackle of yours isn't helping." She moved away from the counter to set her cup in the dishwasher. She sat back down without looking at me and started thumbing through the newspaper, a strained stiffness to her gestures.

"Oh God. Oh no. There's another boy missing." Her mouth drooped like she was about to start sobbing. "Another redhead."

I shrugged. "Something very bad is happening in our town."

She shook her head, covered her eyes with both hands. When she looked up, her gaze was cooler, calculating. "Are you sure you don't have anything to tell me?" Her voice slipped into a whisper.

"I'm not hiding anything."

"You should be careful, Ida. The more you say that, the more it sounds like bull."

***

It was a long, silent car ride. Jade stewing beside me, chewing on her lip like I was about to go down for kidnapping. Murder. Worse. I scrolled through a playlist, earbuds in, avoiding her.

She thought I knew something too. I felt it. Like I was guilty of something just because I stayed quiet.

Whatever.

I wasn't ratting on anyone, and she wouldn't want me to either. No way. Our whole family had it rough, and I wouldn't be the one who got any of us involved in the mess with the cops. No one else saw anything, or they would've already come forward. It wouldn't be me. No way.

It wasn't loyalty. Or fear. It was just . . . Dad.

I didn't want to tell her I saw him that morning. At the house. She'd have freaked. Especially with this new mess about the kid at the pool. She'd go ballistic. Start blabbing to the cops about what Robert said to Mom or whatever. But that's ancient history, and it was all off record anyway. Mom never filed a formal complaint. Besides, it was partly Mom's fault, telling him to go without any notice or anything. It was his home, too, and she was unwilling to forgive. Capital B.

Aunt Jade wasn't even around then. She didn't know anything about how their separation went down. She didn't have a right to an opinion as far as I was concerned.

The truth was, he was really different then. Way different in a messed-up way. He explained everything to me about being preoccupied and distracted by someone else. The stress he was under at work. The trouble drinking was giving him. He never meant to hurt her. Of course he didn't. He loved her. Always loved her. Me and Jade too. The separation was temporary. He promised.

You can't unread a book. That's what he said hard love was like. Problems happened to people, and all a man could do was face them. All of it was just a thing he couldn't undo.

He never meant to hurt us. I couldn't remember what he was talking about, anyway. I was just glad he wasn't upset like that anymore. He hadn't lost his job or anything important.

He just had a new place of his own to sleep. The apartment was really small, but nicer than I expected with a big pool and a workout room. I went there after my shifts at the pool a few times just to hang out. Dad's place was totally safe, and whenever I was there I could be myself. Dad didn't breathe down my neck all the time about consequences and, all caps, The Future like Mom and Aunt Jade. They were the worst. He played it cool all through the separation. And Jade wouldn't ever believe me about back then, what Dad was like. I guess they had a falling out around the time of the separation.

I think it was some 'he said, she said' bullshit. So Jade never believed in him, either. Big B, small itch, like Dad always said. I couldn't wait for her to go back to her own place. She was a trauma junkie.

A tiny impulse quivered inside me. Part of me wanted to admit what I saw to someone about who else was there that day at the pool. Part of me thought maybe I should tell the police. But he asked me not to because of how it'd seem, him being there without anyone knowing. Talking to those boys.

Once he took a couple photos of us at the pool, but only because we looked so much alike. It was just for fun. Nothing creepy.

If I told the cops, they'd ask me more about him. It'd sound bad. Way worse than it really was.

What if they asked stuff I couldn't answer? What he was like as a father. What he was like to Mom before—

Shit. He was nothing but a fling. Not even a speedbump for Mom and Robert. Even when Robert was rotten to her, he wouldn't have hurt her. Any family had problems. The complaints would've told them that already, so I didn't need to. When they split up it was in everyone's best interest. We were all happier. Besides, he would be coming home. They never even legally separated.

Turns out he came home, anyway.

So I couldn't tell anyone about who was there that day. Or at the pool. Not Aunt Jade. She wouldn't get it. Besides, I didn't remember much about those days anyway.

One thing I know is that it'd all make him look guilty. Maybe me too. History is like a book you can't unread.

***

"Not to be gross or anything, but what do serial killers do with little boys?" Colby didn't blink.

God I hated him. He was such a dick. Baiting me. I shrugged. "I don't know. Do you think it matters if they take little boys or girls?"

"Everyone knows that kind of violence isn't about sex, Colby. It's about power." Lala scooted closer to me at the lunch table like it was her way of taking my side.

She had no reason to speak up about this. It wasn't like this was a topic of interest to her. She was simply tuned into my needs. Maybe she sensed he was irritating me. I made good on the moment.

"Right? Maybe we should be asking you that, dude." I pointed at him for emphasis. That made him squirm.

"I'm just saying it's weird that it's been boys. Girl victims are so much more common. That's all. After last year—with your mom." He looked at me straight then, right in the eyes. He let out a honk of a laugh. "Sorry, man, I'm just saying a lot of people in town thought it wasn't suicide, you know? People talk."

"God, shut up!" Lala grabbed my hand under the table. "Don't listen to him, okay?"

"Thanks." I squeezed her hand in mine. "But I got this. Dude, you don't know what you're talking about. What are you trying to do? Convince me my mom was part of some serial killer's grand plan?"

Colby sat back. "No, man. I'm just coming clean with you. The whole town thought it was messed up, the way she died. Maybe she did that to herself, but once this shit with the little boys started—I mean, it's suspicious is all. Like, it's a lot of gruesome for a nowhere town like ours."

Lala threw her hands in the air. "Could you be less aware of how this sounds right now? Because I literally think you are the least sensitive person on the planet."

"It's fine, Lala. He's being honest at least. Do you have anything else you want to say?" I rested my chin in my hands.

"Just seems like whatever nasty shit goes on around here . . . somehow it all comes back to you—doesn't it?"

I sighed.

"What the hell are you saying? That Ida did something to those kids? To his own mom? To anyone? God. The whole town knows Ida and Jade were in school when it happened."

Colby cocked his head at us. Blinked. "Uh huh."

"Because I can totally control what the boys getting kidnapped look like."

"Maybe he's just jealous I dumped him to hang out with you." Lala put an arm around me.

Colby pulled out his phone and started scrolling through messages, acting bored and disinterested.

"Nope. That's not it. You two don't bug me. I just think the situation is weird. The resemblance between you and the missing kids. One of them being from the pool. All this violence all of a sudden. Strange circumstances. Coincidences."

I didn't make eye contact with him. "Strange circumstances? There isn't anything to consider. There aren't even similarities about the cases. Even the cops aren't imagining a connection between these events."

"Right. That's why they keep hauling you in." Colby pointed his phone at me and snapped a picture. I recoiled.

"How do you know the boys are dead?" I blurted it louder than I meant to.

Colby didn't reply right away. He smiled. Probably pleased to get a reaction out of me. He rapped his fingers on the table. "Odds, dude. Playing the odds."

"You want to make bets? You're disgusting." Lala made a gagging sound.

"No. I don't want to make a bet. I mean, what are the odds they're alive after all this time?"

Literally zero. We all knew that.

Lala sucked in a sharp breath. "You're sick."

"Whoever did it had a reason. They always have a reason. I just wonder why they're fixated on kids that look so much like you." He turned the screen around and showed me the picture he just took. "It's got to be freaking you out. It'd be freaking me out."

"There are a lot of possible reasons. Maybe—" I didn't know what to say. "Maybe whoever's doing it— they're just doing it because they can."

Colby cocked his head. Leaned on the table. Lala's expression went blank.

"Maybe they want to prove they are exactly like any other boy."

***

I had to walk away. I pulled a matchbook from my pocket and started lighting them one at a time to relax. I watched each one erupt and simmer to the edge, wondering what it would be like to burn into nothing. To be a boy on fire.

Lighting a match is the sexiest thing I have ever experienced. The way it strikes into flame. The way the heat travels down the stem. It's like holding a tiny explosion in your fingers.

VOYEURS DO IT BEST

Ida Wright, Interview

"**NO! I NEVER** saw my sister fool around with any boyfriends at the pool. That's completely gross. Like I wanted to even think about Jade with someone. Also, Jade is like me. She likes girls."

That got their attention. Maybe they'd watch her now.

"Are you asking her these same questions? Because if you're not, that's kind of sexist, isn't it?" I folded my arms across my chest. Stared at them.

The room was colder than I remembered from the first time I was there. No color. Like if white turned into puke beige and the sun faded it, that was what the walls looked like. On one wall there was a two-way mirror like something out of a dumb cop show. In the center sat a table and two chairs. A plain overhead light hanging from the ceiling that was just bright enough to make my eyes hurt.

"Or is it homophobic because of the stereotype about lesbians being serial killers? I forget. She's always explaining that shit to me." I shrugged. "Maybe it's both. Either way, you lose. You shouldn't be asking me about this. The specificity of the imagery about her is making me highly uncomfortable."

I rapped my fingers on the table. They waited. The same cops who two months ago were all slow and gentle. The short woman with the streaky highlights and the African American guy who probably could've benched pressed me.

"Besides, what does that have to do with anything?"

They gave me a bullshit answer about traumatic events and coping with stress. They suggested they were worried about her. Worried about us both. *Diversions.*

"My sister's not a sl—she's not like that. She doesn't mess around with people." At first, I couldn't tell what they were trying to figure out. Were they accusing me of being a window wanker or a sister-fucker? *Nasty.*

Then I realized they were probing me about *her*. They wanted to know her whereabouts. How much I knew of her daily routine. Who she spent time with. What she did.

Holy shit! Weirdo Jade with the aloof attitude, the stringy hair that covered her eyes, and the patches all over her jacket wasn't just a loner and an outsider at school.

She was one of their suspects.

I decided to play along.

"It's true we've had weird childhoods, but I don't know if I'd call them bad. Our parents had problems but that's normal, right? My dad wasn't really in the picture. Robert forgave Mom. There were some arguments, but nothing rattling."

They nodded. Encouraged me to go on.

"Right, well, they never took stuff out on us, if you mean like hitting or whatever. They weren't violent."

WHAT HAPPENED WAS IMPOSSIBLE

They were pushovers, actually. We ran the house, but I didn't tell them that.

"Yes, I'm sure. I know there were some calls about . . . a thing that happened with my dad—Robert, I mean. But that was a misunderstanding. That should be on the record too. Isn't it? My mom never pressed any charges." I leaned back in the chair.

"I don't know if Jade took it as hard as I did. I mean, she wasn't as close with Mom as me. When Mom—after Mom, she's been even more quiet than usual." I shrugged.

Detective Gutierrez nodded. "Go on."

Hooked.

"Well, she didn't tell me right away about liking girls. Not in a super honest way. She told me she hated the guys at school, then she told me she had a secret. She made me promise not to tell because I guess she thought Mom and Dad would be pissed or disappointed or whatever. That's when she told me about a girl she liked."

They ate it up. Jade the problem child was an obvious solution. This way, they wouldn't ask about Dad. I could protect him from suspicion. When they asked about drugs and alcohol, it was almost too easy.

"She burned her journals in the backyard after. I guess she was worried they were prying or whatever."

"Really?" Melanie scooted in close to the table. "Did she do anything else back there? Drugs, maybe?"

I shrugged. "I'm not sure if she gets high. I mean, not to stereotype or anything, but she looks like it. Doesn't she?"

CAROLINE WRIGHT'S DIARY

May 1

A LOT OF PARENTS worry about their kids. It's part of the job. We sign up for love, but the worry is what kills you. The constant ache that they'll get hurt. You want to protect them from every scraped knee dotting with blood, every disappointment, evert unkind word, every broken heart.

You make bargains. Crazy bargains about the things you'd do to keep them safe. No one can know what that's like unless they've been there.

There's no end to what you'd do for them. God knows it. But you never give up—you can't give up on hope.

You look for signs about those bargains. Dreams. Wishful thinking. Thinking backwards. Once upon a time I was worried because we never had a dog. I worried they never learned about compassion and empathy for others. Then I was grateful we never had a dog because of the things you read about—

I used to worry about the hard times they had at school, why it's so hard for them to make friends. I worried they didn't develop the right—what's the word?—attachments with Robert and I.

I worried about the bonfires we set as a family.

WHAT HAPPENED WAS IMPOSSIBLE

Maybe it was wrong to have so much fun with fire. My goodness, a mother could worry about so many things. It's a wonder anyone ever grows up right when you get down to it. The miracle is that we're not all raising neurotics. Or maybe we are, and that's the realization worth a million bucks! Therapy averted . . .

May 15

I reached a point where I couldn't stand the guilt over the things we couldn't take back. I worried about the things we couldn't do. The separation was hard on us. All of us. Robert's drinking. His affairs. Mine. I wanted him to come home anyway and then I felt guilty about that too. What kind of example was I setting for my own kids? For Ida about how to be a husband one day and for Jade about what to expect from a man? If only!

Sometimes I can't think of a single thing in the universe deeper than my own regret. Why am I filled with so much shame, when I'm not the only one who cheated?

God knows I wasn't a perfect wife to Robert either, but still—was there something I could've done? Something I didn't know about? Something worse than I could stand to consider?

Sometimes I worry so hard about my kids I think it will split me in half. What if someone—not Robert, I know he would never have hurt our babies in that way—but what if a neighbor or coach or teacher had done something. It's unthinkable. These things that cannot be stopped in our world because they are almost invisible. What if something like that could have started all the trouble?

Sometimes you worry about other things too.

What they've done. What they might do. What they're capable of.

***

"That was the entry she made a month ago." Murdock held his hands up, gesturing a question.

"Shit, Warren. I thought you said the journals were a bust."

"They were. Until they weren't. Seems like that kid of hers had some problems."

"Which one?"

Murdock slugged back a mouthful of coffee. "It's vague, but I think she had a problem with the girl."

Mel rubbed her temples. "Damn. It's hard to picture a kid hating their mom enough to do what we saw." Mel coughed. "A girl." She pushed the journal back across the desk.

"Just once I'd love to be surprised, Mel. Just once." He shook his head. "Here's the thing, though. Jay says it was suicide. It's been declared now."

"So why are you showing me all this if it's a closed case?"

"I got a feeling there's more to it, is all. I just—"

"—Want someone else in the loop."

WARNING SIGNS

"WHAT THE HELL, WARREN?" Melanie read the computer screen over Murdock's shoulder. "Who's the serial killer?"

"This was a website Caroline mentioned in her journal. Showed up in her search history, too. I guess she thought—"

"Huh." Melanie tucked a stray hair behind her ear, leaned over for a closer look.

Are you worried your child might grow up to be a serial killer? You're not alone. If you aren't sure about therapists near you, consider a private phone consultation with one of our professionals. If you've begun to ask yourself these questions, this list may help you take an important next step.

Maybe you've noticed the child exhibiting excellent reasoning skills or an interest in assessing the motives of others in an attempt to predict outcomes? Some of the behaviors described below are associated with traits found among serial killers. While individually, they may not be indicative of a concern, taken as a set these are indicators of possible antisocial behavior that merits a serious intervention. These traits do not substitute for medical or behavioral intervention and should only be used as a point of reference.

• Voyeurism. Does the child spy on others or make a habit of watching people, particularly in private moments?

• Shiftlessness. Moving from interest to interest or an inability to commit. In adults this may appear as an inability to hold jobs for any length of time.

• Substance abuse. Numbing behaviors, including turning to excessive drug and alcohol use may indicate a desire to 'disconnect' from reality.

• Child abuse. A past of humiliation and helplessness may be an indicator the child will seek opportunities to feel powerful by inflicting harm to others.

• Poor family life. Weak ties to others, in particular to family of origin.

• Violence toward animals. Widely confirmed, one of the first warning signs of sociopathic tendencies and aggression toward people is often harming animals.

• Arson. A history of fire starting and arson is firmly established as a correlative among violent offenders, particularly serial killers.

Warren massaged the back of his neck. "I wondered what she'd been thinking."

"How long before her suicide was she looking at this?"

WHAT HAPPENED WAS IMPOSSIBLE

"About a month." He closed out the screen.

Melanie took a seat at the desk across from him. "She was worried about one of her kids hurting someone?"

Warren nodded. "It's a strong possibility."

"Is there some other possibility?" Melanie paused. "Tell me what you're thinking."

"Maybe she should've been more worried about herself."

THE FINAL BOY

Aunt Jade

"IDA HAD NOTHING to do with this." *I couldn't believe they were at it again. At this family. At me.*

"We know it's hard to imagine that a young child, a minor could be capable of—" Officer Gutierrez paused, shifted on her feet. "Of hiding something."

Maybe she felt bad about interrogating me. The expression clouding her eyes made me wonder who'd put her up to coming back here.

The detective with her, Murdock, finally broke his silence. "It's hard to consider that someone you think you know so well, let alone a child, may have been involved in a cover up. We aren't suggesting anyone played a role in the kidnapping."

He just barely got the sentence out.

The lady detective scowled at me. *Maybe she'd put him up to this inquisition.* "This is a dead end. You've got to know that. It's desperate."

"Ma'am, we know this isn't easy. We'd like to hear his side of things. Step by step. That's all. How Ida got involved at the pool. Who set up his schedule. Whether or not Jade ever visited him at work. We aren't here to suggest anyone is involved, but Ida was there. He may know something. He may have been unaware of what was happening, but we can't dismiss the possibility that he saw something—something that may turn out to be useful."

That's more like it.

Detective Gutierrez made a production of arranging photos on the table. I didn't look at them or her.

"There are too many coincidences to ignore," Gutierrez said.

"You mean the way he looks? He can't help that. Maybe he's a target! Did you ever bother to think about that? To think about protecting him?"

Was fire shooting out of my nostrils? Probably. Before I went further, I took a deep breath.

"I'm afraid for him. He's upset."

Detective Gutierrez scooted her chair close to the table, her head angled. *I should not have said that.*

"How can you tell? Has he said something?" Murdock asked. *Faking concern.*

I let out another slow breath. "Nightmares. He's having nightmares. He wakes up, yelling. It hasn't ever been this bad. Not since his mother—" *Shit. More I shouldn't have said.*

Detective Gutierrez nodded. Wavy curls bounced around her face. That annoyed me for no real reason. Then it dawned on me. She'd probably come here to question Robert. That's who they expected to find here. Maybe she was the kind of woman to flirt information out of men like my brother. Lonely, good-looking men. Well that wasn't going to work on me. I stiffened, sat up straight.

"He's had nightmares before?" Gutierrez asked.

No point in lying. "Yes. Obviously. He's been through a trauma, and this is bringing it all up."

"Can you tell us more about that? His history of—"

"I can. I don't know the content of the nightmares, of course. I don't pry. But I made sure he saw someone. A professional. After—everything. He keeps a journal now." *Damn it! I shouldn't have said that, either.*

"That's good of you. Sounds like you're a very caring aunt."

"Thank you." *That was more like it.*

"How long have you been living here?" Her voice got quiet. Courteous.

I didn't like her, but Detective Gutierrez was very good at her job.

"I moved in about a month after Caroline's death to help Robert. They've been through a lot, but they're dealing with it."

"And the kids? Do you have concerns about *how* they are dealing with it?" His voice was soft. Nudging me into territory I didn't much like, but he was smooth talking and at least he was trying to be kind.

"Well, who wouldn't? It'd be inhuman not to be concerned. Ida's coping. I think the most significant outcome of those traumatic experiences is that he's mature for his age."

"When you say 'experiences,' do you mean other than his mother?"

I was digging a terrible hole. No way out but through.

"What other experiences?"

"Well, when his father died. He must've told you."

Detective Murdock grunted. They glanced at each other. *Ida hadn't told them.*

"He had a hard time after that." *Why wouldn't he tell them?* "It was very hard to accept. It was hard for them, as a family, but Ida took it badly. He was just getting to know him when . . . " *What could I say without going into the worst of it?*

"Go on."

"Look. Caroline had an affair. It was brief. Ida was a product of that, and they never lied to him. Robert was his dad in every way that counted. They even look alike, when you get down to it."

The woman wrote something in a small spiral notebook then tucked it into her jacket pocket.

"So Ida's biological father wasn't in the picture long?"

"Not really. Ida didn't know the man who—his biological father—very well."

"And Ida's close with Robert?"

"Very close. They're two peas in a pod. In the whole nature-nurture debate, anyone can tell you it's all nurture. He walks and talks just like Robert."

"As for Jade, is Ida jealous of her?"

"Pssh! Hardly. Jade doesn't have much of a bond with anyone." I stopped myself. Pivoted. "I shouldn't say that. She's a teenage girl whose mother died a terrible, tragic death. She doesn't want to talk to her dad about certain things. Girl things, if you know what I mean. Especially now. She's having a hard time."

"For a lot of girls, this is a tough age in the best of circumstances." Detective Gutierrez sounded sincere. For a moment I wondered what her girlhood was like. Pretty as she was, I bet she was the queen of everything or treated like a princess though she had the demeanor of a tomboy. Probably awkward like the rest of us. Still. I appreciated the glimmer of compassion.

"She's my niece. I love her to pieces, but she is a handful. Very aloof. My point is, there's not much for Ida to be envious of with her."

"If he wasn't close to his biological father, what makes you sure he took his death so hard?" Murdock asked.

I hesitated, but I shouldn't have. "Well, it was like closing a door that he hadn't really explored. Sometimes a possibility, a mystery, is romantic. You know kids. Boys. They imagine the best of their fathers, don't they?" *Even that bastard of a man.*

"Sorry to ask, but how did he die?" Gutierrez scowled.

"Right. Well, I'm not sure what to say about his dad. There were questions when he died, but no one was charged with anything. It was assumed to be a suicide." *Just like Caroline.*

"I see. This may sound a little unusual, but Ida seemed to suggest otherwise."

"You mean he didn't mention his dad?"

A shadow seemed to fall across Murdock's face. "Quite the opposite. He mentioned him, maybe by accident. Ida implied his dad had been at the pool. Unless we misunderstood something."

Gutierrez glanced at her partner.

Detective Murdock coughed. "And that it's possible the person talking to him was the final boy that went missing."

The final boy. My head ached. I'd made the mistake of being honest and got a punch in the gut. My mind reeled with what that information might suggest. About Ida.

Not that. I cringed.

"You think he's—" *I couldn't say it. I ran through*

WHAT HAPPENED WAS IMPOSSIBLE

*the alternate conclusions. Anything to avoid the idea
that Ida had become the kind of boy who hurt people.
A monster.* "You're saying he's imagining things? Like
hallucinating? That's impossible."

Gutierrez folded her arms across her chest.
"Either that or he's seeing ghosts."

THAT HAPPENED WAS IMPOSSIBLE

HIS TIME

Ida Wright

THE FIRST TIME was an accident. With Dad. Jumping from the mirror like that. Nobody could've predicted it. The second time I couldn't believe it.

If space was a point on a line—

What happened to them was absolutely impossible. It sure as hell wasn't my fault. I didn't know what I was doing or how. Everything happened too fast. No way I could stop it. I didn't even understand it.

The moment spliced into a series of grisly images. A nightmare.

Time was more of a circle than a linear sequence.

I was in the bathroom downstairs at school. I had asked for a hall pass and walked to the far side of the building just to avoid sitting in class. I was staring at myself. Concentrating on my face in the mirror, looking from different angles like Mom suggested, trying to fix a pose for the class picture. Something to hide the blotch of acne on my chin.

That's when my mind drifted. Thinking about that joke I made in class about fractals. Hiding a body in numbers.

A spectral flash of colorful lights winked when I

opened my eyes. But they were his eyes. A searing pain gripped my limbs. Then everything felt distant and detached. My arms pulled like they'd been anchored with weights. I couldn't control my movement. I squirmed to clench both fists, shake them. I imagined the neurons firing in my brain, attempting even the slightest gesture.

No results. Only a sparking, sulfurous smoke drenched the air, so thick I couldn't see.

First I worried a fuse had shorted, causing an electrical fire in the school bathroom. I scanned the room for burned-out sockets, evidence of something plugged in and forgotten. A stupid mistake that would get someone into a heap of expensive trouble. I coughed, aching to wave a hand in front of my face, but I still couldn't move.

Then a strange image edged into the mirror. It replaced my face, blended into it.

I blinked as smoke cleared. That's when I saw it. The oddly familiar, beautiful face of a strawberry blond woman.

My mother. Caroline. Screaming.

Her face contorted like she didn't recognize me.

In a second she swatted at the air. Then she grabbed the razor. Before I knew it she pawed at the deep gash, blood gushing from her throat. Her curls clung, tangled and matted, to her rouged cheeks. Her lips quivered and contorted. Red lipstick smeared on her front tooth. She attempted to block her face and neck, but something leapt out of the mirror. Grabbed her.

Me. I was doing it. Through her.

A waxy glaze filtered her eyes. She squinted them shut. Hard. Opened.

Did she see me in the mirror? I couldn't really tell.
She clutched Robert's straight razor. Or I did.
Nothing was going to stop what was happening.
Caroline's hand-not-her-hand held the razor to her throat. Pushed. She clung to life, half pulling away, but the press of the blade was irresistibly strong.

She didn't open her eyes while it happened.

I screamed, but no sound came out. The forceful pinch of her ignoring me. The sting of invisibility. For the last time.

Something angry shook inside, froze me in place. Whatever fused our realities in that second, it melded us.

She wasn't Mom then. Just a woman bleeding, losing a battle.

Caroline bled and bled. A wet ribbon drained from the wound on her neck to a thick pool on the tile floor. The fear in her eyes, the smell of too much blood.

I scented it just as clearly as if I'd been there. But I hadn't. Yet I had.

The moment scalded my eyes, like something out of a horror movie. I saw the whole thing. Witnessing any kind of murder was an awful trauma, but watching her, my mother, flinch and wail as she bled to death— that's the kind of pain a guy doesn't get past. It destroyed something inside me. My whole life changed that day because of what I saw. *What I did . . .*

My family was upended. My dad Robert was destroyed. Even my weirdo sister Jade seemed more damaged and aloof than ever.

But I hadn't been there. I couldn't have been there. Caroline was upstairs at home. Alone. I was at school in a bathroom.

Counting. Watching. Pushing.

***

WHAT HAPPENED WAS IMPOSSIBLE

A lot of the gossip landed around my dad. He was the one who seemed suspicious. The recent separation. The neighbors saw the cops there not long before he moved out. The cops interviewed me about it and everything, but nothing stuck to the old man. He was at work. Hell of an alibi. And no way he had the money to hire someone for anything like that. An assassin.

What for? The dumb house was still in his name, anyway. Money was no motive. According to all the expert opinions from therapists to cops and everyone blogging about the case, Robert was worse off without Caroline, not better. No motivation once anyone scratched beneath the surface of the circumstances and the general probability that husbands kill their wives.

I thought Dad was cool, but he fell apart. I didn't expect that. I thought he wanted to move on already. He must've loved her more than I realized. When Aunt Jade moved in to help out, I thought he was nuts. *How fucking pathetic.* Listening to her try to coach us through the pain was even more annoying than listening to him crying in his bedroom at night.

At least Aunt Jade had chops, though. I found that out one morning when she was nagging my sister and me about Mom's death. The three of us were sitting on the kitchen island, pretending to be an un-messy family.

The way I saw it, shared bloodstains and secrets were what made us a family.

"Come on. You know Dad's not an evil genius. He's just a regular guy." Jade rolled her eyes, as usual, then dumped almond milk into her granola and started crunching away.

Fucking hippy.

Aunt Jade chewed her no-calorie puffed air or whatever before it got soggy.

I poured myself a cup of coffee and drank it black. Both of them were alike. Weak in their own ways. Little Jade's predictable rebellions and annoying outrage at the patriarchy and Aunt Jade's concerned, get-in-touch-with-your-emotions bullshit questions.

I decided to call her on it. Ask what she wasn't asking. "It's like you don't trust him. Is that why you moved in here?"

She slurped some of that gross cereal down and chased it with a swallow of milky coffee.

"You're not answering, Auntie. Let's get it out in the open."

Her eyelid twitched and she tensed up, but she didn't say anything right away.

My sister laughed one of those girly nervous giggle things. But when our aunt didn't answer, her face got all serious and mad looking. "Is he right?" she asked.

"Well, it's more like I had concerns about the situation and the strain it put on all of you than any real—" Aunt Jade paused. "It's not like I had seen you very much. It'd been a while, since the separation, and it seemed like a good time to regroup. As a family."

"Oh my god, you think he did something, don't you?" My sister was incredulous. Her voice shrill and loud. "There is no way Dad had anything to do with it." She slammed her empty bowl into the sink. It shattered. She shrank at the sound of the crash, and I could tell she didn't mean to break the dish.

Just when I thought she was getting tough.

"Young lady, I am here because I care about you.

Both of you." Aunt Jade pursed her lips. "Are you going to clean up that broken glass?"

My sister was already picking the shards out of the sink. Apologetically. *Wuss.*

"You're not exactly answering, though—are you, Auntie?"

Aunt Jade's expression hardened until it puckered into wrinkles. She looked a million years old.

"When the police started asking questions, which were perfectly reasonable, by the way, it seemed prudent to step in in case—he was detained. I didn't think my brother killed Caroline. I never thought that." Her voice wavered.

It was a little unconvincing the way she spit out the words.

"Sometimes couples end up in places they don't expect," she said.

My sister scoffed. "What would you know? You're not married."

That impressed me. "Damn, Jade!" I couldn't help but laugh.

"It may surprise you that I know about all kinds of things. Caroline and I were really like sisters. She told me about the—about why your dad moved out, about the stress they'd been under. I know Robert loves—sorry—*loved* her very much. But love doesn't always prevent people from doing or saying terrible things. Things you can't take back."

"Like murder?" I asked.

"No. I never thought he killed her."

She said it smoothly this time. Like she believed it.

Aunt Jade stammered. "I understood that the police might take up that angle. There were reasons to wonder. And I didn't want you two ending up in the middle of a worse mess than necessary."

Whatever. She wasn't here because she cared about her brother. She was here to keep an eye on us. To make herself feel better. *How thoughtful of her.* So she was a narcissist, like everybody else.

II.

AN UNREMARKABLE MAN

A YOUNG MAN
WITH PROBLEMS

Jade's Observations

NOTHING CAME EASY for Ida. That was the first lesson. Eventually, he learned that all the way to his bones.

Like that time in high school. Ida never should've asked the biology teacher how long it took to drain a body. Curiosity raised red flags.

Mr. Kaye probably wagged a finger at him. "That's the kind of question that could get you in trouble, kiddo." Mr. Kaye had a way with words.

The class got back to work after a brief, awkward silence. Apparently, the answer to that particular question also depended on the artery. Minutes or hours. I heard about the incident by lunch.

Word travels fast. Good to know.

Despite the odd-pitched humor he wore like a badge, I knew he carried a brightness that was a magnet of sorts, though not for what most guys craved. He was tall and lanky with wavy hair, pale skin, sky-blue eyes. He had a cherubic face despite a few splotches of acne on the chin.

He was a smidge too innocent looking, so no one ever asked him out on a date. Instead, Ida was the fallback guy. The confidant. That was something. He knew when to offer a smile, how long a supportive hug should last, and when to spring for a plate of cafeteria fries after someone cried on his shoulder. I couldn't figure out how'd he know what to do because at home he never seemed to care about anything or anyone.

At first, people talked about us because of the tragedy, but Ida got a reputation for bad taste. Things like that blood joke. Gags like that stuck in high school. They made him kind of popular. His incongruent personality was a piece of luck. It gave him an angle of humor that slid into any situation like a hot, sharp knife.

Later that same week Henry, the basketball star and future prom king, dumped Ida's best friend Sasha. When a bucket of red paint poured out of Henry's locker, everyone knew who did it. Nobody ratted him out.

"Damn that boy is sick." That's what they said.

"Very *Carrie*," Ida said. Everyone laughed.

"I couldn't imagine a better friend." Sasha slapped him on the shoulder. People in the hall moved on. Meanwhile I moved through the same hall like a ghost. Ida didn't even speak to me at school. He just ignored me to death.

Earlier in the year when the other thing in statistics class happened, everyone got it. People talked about it for weeks, but they didn't take it seriously. It was just Ida and his weird jokes. He could say anything. Here's what I heard.

"You can hide anything in numbers." Ms. Johnston tapped examples onto the chalkboard. She was talking about fractals.

Someone in the back of the room startled awake. Not Ida. Ida was riveted.

WHAT HAPPENED WAS IMPOSSIBLE

"Like a body?" Ida's innocent smile, those rosy pink cheeks blooming with splotches.

Ms. Johnston turned around. One hand on her hip, head cocked. An eruption of giggling and sighs. "Ida, is that a real question?"

Ida didn't answer right away. Ms. Johnston tapped her foot. Ida's face flushed. Everybody else laughed. His classmates always knew when to laugh.

Still. That's when it started. He locked himself in his room. Lost hours. Counting methodically. I heard him chanting like the numbers were a mantra. Detached.

Contemplating it, I bet. Drunk on the notion. Hungry for it.

I didn't want the kind of attention he got, but still. I was there. Watching him get it from everyone. Making them laugh.

But I saw him at home. Even if I didn't know his motivation, I knew his hobbies and habits. I knew where he came from, and I knew he was hiding something other than an offbeat sense of humor.

IDEAL NUMBERS AND THE PRIVATE ABYSS

Ida

WHAT COULD I put into a number, what could I pull out?

The question was how to manipulate things around me. If I could figure it out—*how to get inside of a number*.

Cracking a number could open up a portal of sorts. In and out. I stared into a mirror, focused on one pupil. The edges of it like tiny mirrors folding deeper and deeper into a cold abyss.

Fractals.

If I got in, could I get out? Where would I end up?

I concentrated hard. This was the math of opportunity. I believed in myself. Someone would do this, why not me? I could be the one to understand the infinite curve of time, how to bend it, how to reshape space with a series of deductions. *Concentrations.*

I would build an equation built on a new understanding of physical laws.

What could I hide with that?

Then there was high school. That's how it was. Friends and fantasies. An occasional beer. Late nights, greasy pizza, bad movie festivals.

WHAT HAPPENED WAS IMPOSSIBLE

In a crowd, I made people laugh. That was especially helpful when I overshared or spoke too much about certain things. I embraced the quirky. Offered some harmless fun. Wore it like a badge of individuality.

I was a peculiar sort of person. I got the benefit of the doubt for the price of a smile. Teachers called me smart but distractible. Classmates said I was easy going and likable. Never mind what my sister said about me.

Everything depended on a key assumption about my good intentions. My presumed goodness built a parameter of safety, a harmless, snide coating for my bloody remarks.

Ida had a bad sense of humor. Ida had a mean streak but never meant to hurt anyone. He was bright, though sometimes his choices bordered on inappropriate. Ida didn't know when to quit.

Those were the kinds of things grownups said. Truth was, they didn't want to look too closely. The benign neglect of social expectations.

But the point was, nothing came easy for me. People saw that. They felt for the obstacles, they imagined what stood in my path. Especially after Mom died.

They knew I had a lot of battles.

A deadbeat drunk of a bio-dad. Two suicides. Those were real problems. Living with a guy who was questioned about his wife's suspicious suicide. The stench of accusation and bad luck clung to the family somehow.

Poor Ida! Empathy rocked.

No one could outrun the odds of that kind of pain forever.

E. F. SCHRAEDER

It made sense that I wanted to disappear into the logical world of the mind, into the numbers. Forever.

Once I saw what they could do I wanted more.

"Become an accountant," my guidance counselor said.

"Follow your heart," Aunt Jade said.

"Trust yourself," Robert said.

And I did.

A GROWN MAN

BY THE TIME Ida was twenty-six years old he'd accumulated a small but sizable mass of wealth. Fifty percent of which was based on the kind of good luck that depended on someone else's very bad luck. Ida knew his way around the numbers, and snapped up the chance to buy a house sized for six people, thirty miles from his hometown.

Thirty miles.

That was exactly far enough. The recognition of a traumatic past wasn't daily, but predictable. Ida leaned on it anytime he needed a dose of attention, a splash of adrenaline.

"When my mom died—god, you probably heard about it . . . " He'd wait.

His relatable, sad bits of information served as convenient decoys when he met someone. A potential date, though he hadn't really had a relationship since college. Everyday promised a walk on the campaign trail of being his best self. Living up to his potential. He vowed not to settle for just anyone. He needed someone who saw what he saw. More miracles than excuses.

Sometimes, after a nudge, he started at the beginning. He'd explain how his biological father died. Alone in the garage. Ida a kid in high school.

Then his mom a year later. Reminding anyone who'd listen how hard his life was.

A dead father. People cared right away about that kind of thing. At least that's how it seemed. That kind of pain counted for something.

A familiar longing. He needed his biological dad, and he'd never get to know him. Robert was a good guy and all, sure, but a man needed a father.

When his mother died, the poor kid seemed lost in tragedy. It went like that for a while. Easy encouragement and understanding through high school. Then college. Lots of steady support.

Then he grew up. Expectations changed.

As a businessman, his talent for astute timing never caused much concern. He required less sympathy, more action. Instead of affirmation and apologies he got lucky breaks sealed with handshakes and smiles. He handled other people's emotions like a calculator managed equations. Quick efficiency. The pure math of emotional manipulation in his pocket like a tool.

Things started going his way.

INHERITANCE

Ida Wright, at home

"YOU'RE LUCKY."

"That's my middle name." Ida smirked, palming the key from Daniel, his dad's estate lawyer. "I honestly never thought I'd be back here. I'm surprised he had money to keep the place all these years. Even like this." He shook his head. "I must've told him a hundred times to downsize. Get into a nice condo or something. He wouldn't listen."

"Fathers can be sentimental." Daniel said. "Besides, you can't really go home again."

Ida didn't respond.

"I mean it's probably different than you remember."

"Well, thanks for meeting me here."

Daniel didn't move.

"Unless you want to help me clean up, I guess that's it." Ida stood in front of the door.

"Right. Well, let me know if you have questions about any of the filings or outstanding contracts."

"Outstanding contracts?"

"Your dad hired a few other contractors to keep things up. He didn't tell you?"

"That's Dad. Why call me when he could hire someone else." Ida shrugged.

"He'd been struggling. Maybe it was a point of pride."

Ida's arms stacked at his chest. "If there was a judgment of me in there, I'm not feeling it. I travel for my jobs. I told him I couldn't help out. Not here. I don't know why he hung onto a place he couldn't take care of. After everything that happened here." Ida paused for dramatic effect. "He must've mentioned—"

"No, he never. Oh—that Wright family."

"Yep. The street of a well-publicized suicide. All those years ago."

"Sorry."

"Thanks."

"Didn't you have a sister?"

"Jade. Yes. She's not really part of the family anymore. Dad wasn't—what do they call it? Progressive about her lifestyle choices, so I guess—"

"Ah. So that's why she wasn't mentioned in the will."

"Harsh, huh?" Ida chuckled. "I'll let her know. Or not."

"Well, it's all yours, now. You may want to expect some calls from collection agencies. Since the hospitalization he probably missed some payments."

"Whatever it is, I'll take care of it. As usual." His ears warmed, reddening.

Daniel stood there like he expected an invitation to enter. Ida didn't offer one.

"Well, thanks again, Danny."

Daniel cringed. "Great. Good luck." He headed back to his car.

"Of course." Finally, Ida opened the door to the time capsule of his dad's life.

Former life.

WHAT HAPPENED WAS IMPOSSIBLE

One foot hovered on the threshold.

Where I found what the numbers meant. What they could do.

Ida set a foot inside.

However improbable, a dense shock of familiar scents drenched him. He closed his eyes, conjuring a tunnel to childhood. He inhaled the soapy aroma of his dad's laundry detergent, a hint of cigars though the old man swore he hadn't smoked in a decade. A strong dose of garlic and herbs seemed to have leaked into the walls, like tomato sauce was the only thing Robert ever cooked.

One, two three Ida took the steps quickly. Upstairs held the denser memories of another scene. A bite of power. The scent of blood.

Beneath that, Ida picked up something deeper. Sour and familiar. Comfortable. The smell of death.

Ida exhaled hard. *Time to get on with it.* He headed back downstairs.

The place was exactly as he remembered it. The same old blue couch, fading to gray and unmoved along the wall, his dad's rump-slump in the corner cushion. A mirror hung in the hallway with his mother's gold cross dangling from the corner—the one she never removed from her neck when she was alive. *The one she wore on the day she died.*

"Full circle."

Ida looped the chain around a finger and lifted it, letting the cross swing like a hypnotist's pendulum. After inspecting the karats on the back, he clenched it into his fist. "This is mine now, too." He slipped it into the chest pocket of his jacket.

Everything was better in his own place. Shinier somehow. Maybe he'd sell it off fast, maybe he'd make a few changes and flip it for even more cash. Maybe this would be the start of something new. Something good.

Ida considered his mother, still memorialized around the house. Her color choices, her furniture, her decisions. Her framed face watched him from the mantle. "Jesus, how the hell did he stand her?"

As a boy, Ida sat at the piano hammering out a song furious and fast, his fingers blurring. He closed his eyes, swaying so hard that curls of hair fell into his eyes. His hands were almost clumsy fumbling across the keys, the vivid sound and thrumming vibrations. When he finished, he started right back again. Over and over, he played so that the floor shook, and although the tune wasn't a catchy one, soon the whole family learned it. Nonstop until his mother came into the room, hovering.

She was a large woman. The word lumbering had been used more than once by strangers. An angry head-shake as she stood behind him.

"Ida." She said it only once, but sharply.

He stopped banging on the keys and returned to practice one of the impossible concertos assigned by the boring busy body piano teacher Miss Something or Other who didn't understand that his fingers were simply too bulky and coarse for the delicacy demanded by such impossible notes. He hated practice hour and preferred free play, when his creativity was set loose. Like with numbers.

Now the piano was his, and the house too. With them both gone and his sister cut out like a tumor, everything was all his.

He took a seat at the bench. Craned his neck like he was listening for an echo of that old tune, but the memory was out of reach. He could've really learned to play if she'd let him. He could've been great, but Caroline hadn't let him explore his full potential. She never believed in him.

At least all that was behind him now. And his whole life awaited him, too. Freedom.

Ida sat down at the piano. It was out of tune, but he played anyway. The melody he invented as a boy came back to him slowly.

She was wrong about the song. It was mesmerizing and wonderful. It was his.

"I remember the tune easier than your face, Mother." Ida spoke to the stale air of the empty room. He rapped his fingers on the piano. It wasn't hard to imagine her listening. An angry ghost trapped where she died. Where he killed her.

Something stirred in him. Not sadness or a yearning for forgiveness. Just memories shaken loose by the familiar surroundings.

Melodramatic or gothic potential aside, perhaps music was more like math than any other form of expression. Maybe the melody provided an axiom— symbolic value and emotion. A kind of container.

He slammed the piano lid closed, enjoyed the crack of the wood. Returning might've been a bad idea. Staying too long could quell his luck. Ignoring the possible risk wasn't practical.

Ida had to sell. Ditch the past along with it. Move on.

Ida called Monica Sedgewick, the hotshot realtor he worked with on a land deal an hour north. Monica, a one-time rival and current ally with benefits, was a sharpshooter when it came to money. She'd snuck in and undercut him once on a deal, and he'd been careful to keep people like that on his side, especially women. He wouldn't let it happen again. He decided the sale of the family home should be quick and quiet. No need to stir things up. He called a mover and arranged for the piano to be delivered to his house within the week.

***

Ida met Monica at a meeting that didn't go his way.

"I just said that." Ida glanced around the table, staring at the relaxed faces of everyone at the meeting. Everyone but him.

Then came the hideous peal of laughter. The cackle plowed through Ida so swiftly, so surely that he wanted to cover his damned red ears. He would've but for the shock waves flowing through him.

In his stomach, nothing but a rotten group of butterflies. No steely strength, not a glimmer of optimistic kindness. He gulped a breath and pricked up his chin. *Be bigger than this.*

"I know what I said." Ida pulled his hands onto his lap. *None of them heard me.*

"Anyway, let's get back on topic." Sedgewick glanced at him, he knew she had. He felt her eyes on him. *Laughing eyes.* "Before things go offtrack any further."

Sedgwick's eyes were cold as marble.

She'd regret that.

Ida kept his eyes on the presentation after that and his mouth shut. But he balled his hands into tight fists under the table, knuckles whitening. That was the one contract his firm didn't get, and it pissed him off.

She pissed him off. Ida was the last to move when they finished the meeting. When Monica asked him to hang back, stepping aside after everyone else left, he was shocked cold.

"Could we have an abridged conversation about this?" Sedgewick's painted fingernails tapping the table. Her neat hair in pretty, black curls around her face.

"Like a post-mortem?" Ida stood up. Looked her in the eyes.

"Something like that, yes." She smiled.

She was pretty when she smiled.

"Sure. Shoot." Ida dared her to challenge him.

"Well, here's the thing. You're in business. I'm in business. Let's not mince words."

"Great. Go on."

"You were pretty hostile in there. Seemed like you took the loss of this bid pretty personally."

Ida shrugged. "You're direct."

"I don't like to bullshit people. You didn't get this one, but I like your style. You're direct, too. I want us on the same side of the table at some point. Soon."

Ida wondered if his boyish charms were at work. "Let's make it happen." He smiled.

"Good. I'd like to know what that was about then. The anger."

Ida sighed. "I'm at a point in life where I can't imagine anything but violence in rooms like this. It's about taking. That's always hostile. It's a question of where I write it in, you know?"

She pulled back. "I think it'd be a good idea to give this some thought, Ida. You sniped at me. It was like a bomb going off in there. Maybe it'd be a good plan to work on your timing."

"My timing is perfect. That's not it. Not quite. I mean it's embedded in the point of view. Something I'm just keen to include."

"What is?"

"In any transaction, it's the violence of it I like. It's like I have to just do something. I'll make people see me. To take me seriously, I mean." His voice inched higher again, nearly booming.

Monica took a step back.

"I'm passionate about the numbers, Monica. You've got to see it my way." His voice pitched irrationally again just like at the meeting. His cheeks went pink and his mouth twisted into a tight knot of frustration.

Bitter and puckered. Like a child, a pouty, ugly child.

Monica tensed. "There you go again. This is the kind of thing you should try to avoid, Ida."

"I have to do something!"

"You're not thinking it through, Ida. To do business with me—"

She sounded like his school counselors. Like his professors. Like his exes. Like a hundred other people who just didn't see him or understand. "My point of view is different, okay? This is what I am. I'm enthusiastic!"

Monica's posture changed. Minutes ago she was a ruthless broker, but she'd softened. She liked getting a rise out of him. He could smell it.

Monica deliberately, slowly unfolded her arms, dropped them to her sides. "Can you imagine bringing something else to the negotiating table? Something other than this kind of enthusiasm?" She leaned her head sideways, tuning into him like a radio station.

The open posture of an invitation.

Ida widened his stance. "No. I mean sometimes I lack the imagination to effect anything else."

WHAT HAPPENED WAS IMPOSSIBLE

"Well, that's good to know." Monica crossed the room, moving away from him. She stopped at the door, then turned to face him. "There may be times where that kind of energy is useful." She smiled.

He really looked at her then. Not like a business opponent, but like a woman. "So we're on? You'll keep me in mind?"

"I think I will."

"It'd be hard not to. I've got some influential ties. You won't be disappointed." Ida grinned. "You know if you need someone to push an agenda, I can do it."

She reached out for a handshake. "And that's how you turn a threat into an ally."

FROM ADVERSARY TO FUCK-BUDDY

Monica Sedgewick, Realtor

I KNEW HE wanted me. But in the same way he wanted power. It was never about companionship. Anyone could see that.

I promised myself not to fall for him, but whenever we were near each other, I sensed something potent. I wasn't even sure if I liked it. But I didn't mind the attention, and I enjoyed the sex.

Was that so wrong?

That's the problem with romances, with the whole script. Always telling men to fight for the girl, and telling women to fight for the impossible. If this were one of those movies, I'd fall for him no matter what. But ours wasn't that kind of movie.

I wasn't sure what kind of movie it was.

Damn, I hoped I wasn't lying to myself. Stalling joy. Standing in my own way, blocking the good things that were there for the taking.

I knew one thing about Ida Wright. When he called, I always picked up. When he asked, I always said yes. Even if I made him wait.

He asked about flipping a house. Nothing sexy. I told him I'd get there as early as I could, but I lied. Ida was ripe for a lesson in patience.

WHAT HAPPENED WAS IMPOSSIBLE

***

Ida was pacing the sidewalk in front of a grubby house on a cul-de-sac. His crisp two step, checking his watch and scowling like he had a grudge against the place.

His face was a little reddened, either from the chilly air or his mood.

"Finally!"

He yelled the second I opened the door to my Lexus.

"You on lady time or what?"

"Don't be an asshole. You know I don't do residential. This wasn't a priority. I had to squeeze it in between meetings, and you're lucky I'm here."

"Lucky. So everyone keeps saying." He crossed his arms in front of his chest. "You're touchy today. Let's cut the shit. Like a guy can't even be satirical with you."

I appraised the place. It wasn't much to look at. Peeling paint, old windows. No curb appeal. "Right. So this is the joke it looks like?"

"Correction, not touchy. I'd say we've reached bitchy." He laughed, like that made it okay to call me a bitch. Anything I said to correct it and I was too sensitive, too PC. "Look, it's a family house, okay? I want to dump it, and I figured your team would make the most of it."

That was unexpected. "You grew up here?"

"Hooked, huh?" He opened his arms wide. "Yep. This is where all the magic started."

That grin of his. God he was handsome when he smiled.

"You didn't come from much, did you?"

"I didn't lie. Nothing came easy for me. Not really and not ever." He smiled again. Clicked his tongue at me. Shrugged. "All part of my charm."

E. F. SCHRAEDER

All of a sudden Ida was showing me who he really was. Underneath all the bluster and bluff. He was getting real with me. Maybe I was hooked.

LEARNED HELPLESSNESS

Jade Wright

I WAS INVISIBLE back then. Ida's little sister. Didn't matter what I did or where I was, that's what people said.

Even when our mom died, everyone catered to him. I'm not complaining. I'm an introvert. I didn't want the attention. But still. I noticed. He had a way of capturing the focus the way a magnifying glass collects sunlight.

I wasn't sure what he did with it, where he pointed the energy he drew. Not to carry the metaphor too far, but it wasn't hard to imagine a crisped pile of ants, dead in the wake of him.

I didn't want it to be true, but I knew it was. Ida was capable of anything. Everything. Yes, including murder. Torture.

All these years later now I still wondered about him. I knew the state of the bodies they found. I knew, but couldn't explain how. I wasn't sure what to say to my friend Jones, the cop, but I had to say something. I invited her to my place for coffee. Something casual where nobody but her would hear what I had to say.

"What if someone had a hunch? Do you listen to that sort of thing?"

"At this point? Sure. What do you have?"

"It's about my brother."

"The asshole?"

"The one and only."

"I'm listening."

"I think he may have something to do with what's been happening. The murders. The women."

"Whoa, Jade. That's a leap." She took a sip of coffee.

"I know it's messed up, but I think he's behind it somehow. He was always there. When things went bad."

Jones took my hand in a very cop way, comforting me. "Have you considered the events might be triggering you?"

I pulled my hand away. "That's not it. Don't turn this into a mental health thing."

"Sorry, it's just—I can only imagine this brings a lot up."

"Sure it does. Memories of what it's like to grow up with a sociopath brother are pretty unforgiving."

"Okay. I'm listening. Tell me." Jones went total cop face. Blank expression, all ears.

"I'm not going to lie. I want him to get what's coming to him. After all this time, I want him to pay for it. For everything."

"You're skipping the part about why you think it's him."

"Right. Sorry. It's not just a hunch. He always gave me the chills, you know? And I saw him doing things when we were kids. Weird shit. Watching himself in the mirror. I'd hear him at night counting. For hours."

"Counting?" Jones pulled a face.

"I know, but it was creepy as fuck, okay? The numbers. When I read about the numbers on the victims' foreheads it just took me to Ida. I can't explain it. Something about those memories of him counting in the dark like he was practicing at something."

"You're talking like, what? Magic?"

Incredulous. Of course she was. Jones was about facts. Empiricism. Evidence.

"No. Not magic. Something else."

"Well, that's helpful, Jade."

"Isn't it? Ida's a person. Everything in the papers says no leads. I'm giving you one. Can you just look into it? Check his whereabouts or whatever it is cops do?"

Jones snorted. "Sure. Childhood memories, feelings, tips from friends about a serial killer. Why not?" Chin in her hands, elbows on the table. Jones shook her head. "It's not like we have anything else."

"I'll tell you one thing. Whoever she is, when Ida selects someone, she doesn't stand a chance. Not once he decides."

That's how my childhood went, then adolescence. Tragedy. Bloodshed. Recovery. I pushed through, but Ida lingered, absorbing it all.

"The real mystery is why everyone believes he's such a good guy."

UNCONFESSED

Detective Jones

IDA WRIGHT SAT in the holding cell as still as a block of ice. For well over thirty minutes, the man barely twitched. Not a crease in the brow. Not a single drop of sweat. Hands flat on the table, his hazel blue eyes unfazed, a smirk on his face.

I studied everything about that face. Ida had short blondish hair cut neat as a pin close to the scalp, with a little flip of bangs gelled to stick up in a very intentional twirl. *What kind of guy takes the time to style his hair before coming to the police station for questioning?*

I'd call him actively nondescript. An ultimately average, middle aged white guy with a smooth complexion. No sags under the eyes. No fatigue. No signs of stress at all. He wore a crisp blue button-down shirt and a pair of jeans. He carried just enough paunch to look more like a contracted boss than a day laborer.

Sitting across from him I noticed that he even smelled nice, with a clean, cedar musk cologne tinting the otherwise stale air. I forced a half-smile.

"Coffee?" I extended a green paper cup in his direction as I sat down.

"No thanks. What's going on here, officer . . . ?"

"Jones."

"Can I be of help with something?" He scratched at his earlobe until it reddened.

Polite as pie. That smirk got on my nerves. The more I questioned him, the cooler he got.

Jade was right. Ida was guilty.

Before long, we all knew it. There just wasn't any evidence. Not a stitch. We'd brought him in on a gamble, hoping being interviewed with several women in the room might trip him up, reveal a trace of the hostility he held for his victims, possibly for all women. Instead all we had was a principle of presumed innocence. That and the hunch that if we let him go, he'd claim another life.

At the precinct, none of us had figured out his type. In three weeks, four women were dead without a clear pattern. Each victim came from a different employment field, ethnic background, neighborhood, and social group. No obvious ties between the women other than falling between the ages of thirty and fifty-five.

Only one thing linked the cases beyond a doubt. Each victim had a number scrawled on their foreheads in red lipstick. Same shade. Crimson Lust.

It started with "2," but after "3" it jumped to "5." Maybe there were undiscovered victims. Maybe it was a game. Or maybe the killer was into math. Or numerology. Like Jade suggested.

We had earned some very bad press lately, so we brought in profiler Liz Pine just before news of the third murder broke. Panic was already growing throughout the city thanks to a worried mayor stoking a media frenzy.

By then, my best friends Violet and Jade had been

unofficially consulting, way off the record. At first, I planned to keep it that way. Jade being related to a suspect didn't help and neither of them had a criminal background. But that was only half of it. Involvement could've made either of them a potential target.

Through my dad's heart attack and Violet's divorce, we three had a bond that conquered hard times and skepticism. A psychic and an estranged sister working as a part-time philosophy professor wouldn't have much credibility among the police. For that matter, introducing them wouldn't have helped my reputation on the task force either. Even I might've dismissed "visions" if they'd come from anyone else, but I trusted Violet. And Jade had uncanny insights about what motivated people—regardless of any ill will she harbored for her brother.

Most of the time Violet kept those psychic skills to herself when it came to active investigations. But she called me one morning with vivid details. Details that hadn't been released to the press, and the conversation became productive. Violet mentioned a white motorcycle and a rented Winnebago. The tire tracks she described matched what we found at the scene.

With a little prodding, Violet's insights got me talking to Jade again. She didn't discuss her brother much, but she said he always seemed capable of worse than anyone suspected. Turns out, Ida rented a vehicle that lined up with a car that'd been spotted nearby.

When I told Jade we talked to Ida, a note of relief in my voice, she told me two things.

"Trust me, he'll have a loose alibi and a squeaky-clean persona."

WHAT HAPPENED WAS IMPOSSIBLE

"Now you're psychic?" I asked.

"Our whole family is riddled with suspicious deaths. He's always at the center of every disaster. Trust me. I know him," she said.

She wasn't wrong.

Wright claimed to be out riding his Harley on the evening in question, said there'd be a bartender who could roughly confirm his whereabouts at Capers. *A white motorcycle.*

Just like Jade suggested, Ida offered up an alibi that was as verifiable as it was rehearsed.

Violet and Jade were spot on. So much for my rigorous investigative skills.

Ida didn't disappoint. By the end of the interview, everyone on the task force had the same hunch. Something about him was off. He was our guy.

Proving it was my problem.

UNLIKELY COHORTS

Jade Wright, sister of suspect

I DIDN'T GO to bars because I didn't drink anymore. And the last thing I wanted to do was celebrate. Violet and Jones insisted. Our hunches delivered Ida to the cops. Make a quick toast with some club soda and go home.

Three women, three glasses. A few encouraging words. Thirty-five minutes tops. I walked through a gauntlet of smokers and vapers clustered around the front door. Inside the air still clung heavy with smoke. My friends were already there at a table in the back.

"I want you two to help on the case," Jones said.

I laughed so hard I spit out a mouthful of club soda.

Violet let out a squeaky laugh. "Oh, that's rich. A cop asking a psychic for tips. I'm not FBI approved, you know." Violet tipped a beer my way. "What's that snotty Liz going to think of me?"

"Not much would be my guess. Not much at all." Jones rapped on the table. "Don't care."

Violet leaned back on a barstool. "Look, I don't want to be indelicate, but do you guys pay a stipend or a consulting fee for this sort of thing? It's been a lean couple of months."

"Oh, I—you know what, I don't know. I'll look into it, though. Sorry. I didn't know. Business slow?"

WHAT HAPPENED WAS IMPOSSIBLE

"At the salon? Yeah. People tend to get their haircut less often when they don't have any money."

"I'll look into it. You're okay, right?"

For a psychic, Violet kept a lot of things to herself.

"Sure, I'm fine, but when it comes to suburbia's finest, well, you know what I mean. Can't trust them, myself, but I'd love to take their money," Violet said.

"Are you selling your soul to the devil?"

"Thanks for that, Jade."

Jones cringed. "I want Violet right there beside me whether some hot shot profiler likes it or not. I'll find the money if I have to pay you myself."

"Just like that, you've got a psychic on the task force." I held up my club soda for a toast. No takers.

"As for you, he's your brother. I need to know everything you know about him."

"Not cool, Jones."

"Gratis, I guess. Shit, that's half my usual rate." I set the half-finished drink on the table. "No blood money needed. We adjuncts live on student loan debt and good intentions."

Whether or not Jones liked it, at least we were candid about our lack of faith in the police force. The optics were worse than usual. OCPD had been investigated for corruption not five years ago. They adopted de-escalation models and crisis interventions, probably for cover, but change came slow. The worst of it cascaded from an incident with an unarmed Latino boy last month who was injured while being questioned over a B.S. nuisance call. The officer in question was fired after mishandling the whole situation. The kid might've been physically okay, but the incident was an unacceptable example of traumatizing cowboy-cop shit that needed a hard stop. I'm pretty sure if the three of us hadn't been friends before the news broke, we wouldn't have become friends afterwards. Now the town had a serial killer hunting women and no leads. Like I said. Bad optics.

That the best lead on this string of murders had come not from their work but a psychic's hunch and my own elusive memories of my brother? I'm sure that tidbit was just going to have to stay Jones' secret. A killer was on the loose, and I just got recruited to the team trying to bring justice to my brother, the escape artist.

THE PSYCHIC

Violet, the Consultant

I HAD TO make a good first impression with the OCPD. Ironies never cease. I picked my most conservative tan suit, white shirt, hair pulled back in a tight ponytail. Boring, but professional.

"Liz, this is my friend Violet," Jones said. I bit down on my lip, hard. I gave Liz a sideways glance.

"Violet the psychic." Liz looked me up and down.

"That'd be me." I winked at Jones. Liz was attractive, and Jones hadn't mentioned that. I guess she's the opposite of psychic, whatever that is.

"Well, nice to meet you, Violet, but I'm going to be the resident skeptic, okay?" Liz said.

Honesty. Nice. "Sure thing. I'm a bit of a skeptic myself. It's hard to believe in much these days, but hey, if you believe in the criminal justice system, I can believe in my own insight."

"That settles it. We're all having lunch," Liz said.

"Well shut my mouth. I've never been more surprised," Jones said.

"Guess that's why you're not the psychic, huh?" I smiled at Liz.

All in all, that introduction landed as a success. No one's toes were stepped on, and we all showed a sense of humor. No one entered the Land of Woo, not even me. As for Ida, all three of us agreed he remained the main suspect.

"We can watch him to a point, but that's it. Until we have more to go on, we can't justify heavy surveillance. I bet he's the type who'd complain," Jones said.

"About these hints you get, is there any way to tie them to the next victim?" Liz asked.

"Jesus! What if he's done?" Jones' expression soured.

"The numbering. He's got to have a personal reason or it's too random," Liz said. "I bet he's going for ten minimum, some kind of a numbered list, or something we haven't figured out yet."

"That makes utterly no sense. It could be the seven deadly sins . . . "

"Numbered lists." I started counting my fingers. "Numbers are infinite."

Liz's jaw tightened.

"Why ten?" I said.

"Maybe she's psychic." Jones laughed.

The waitress set down our food. Tossed salads for me and Jones. Falafel platter for Liz.

"Thanks." I smiled at the waitress. She seemed happy enough to ignore me, staring at Liz.

Liz didn't notice. "No, seriously, Ida is a perfectionist. His shirt was pressed, his hair was precise. Even his nails were filed and neat. Everything about him screamed uptight. A guy like that'd have a reason for the odd numbering pattern. Either we haven't found the others or he's got another meaning for the numbers." She paused, chewing on her bottom lip.

"Huh. So, it's not a decoy. It's a message?"

"That's my hunch," Liz said.

"Let's hope there aren't more undiscovered victims out there," Jones said.

"Let's hope we fucking catch him." Liz slammed her hand down on the table so hard our dishes shook. The people at the tables around us glanced over and pretended not to notice.

"Sorry. So Violet, how does your particular . . . talent work?"

I couldn't tell if Liz was trying to make nice or change the subject. It didn't much matter to me.

"Honestly, I'd have to say they're usually like waking dreams. Visions." Jones pushed some romaine leaves around her plate then stabbed at a sun-dried tomato.

"She's never wrong. I mean it," Jones said. "I know it sounds crazy but every single time, she's on the nose. She's the real deal."

"I know it sounds hokey, but it's what happens. I get glimpses, flashes, you know? And it's like I can't unsee them. This time, with him, I wished I could. I've never seen anything like this before."

"Bad?" Liz asked.

Jones flushed. "Shit. I never bothered to ask. What a jerk."

I ignored Jones' revelation. "This one's brutal. I'm seeing the things in his house, or wherever he's doing it. The things in his head. He's a complete sicko. He lives to do this, to torture. He's been studying serial killers for years. A real hobbyist." I pushed my plate away. "It turns my stomach."

"I'm sorry to push you into this." Liz patted my hand.

"You're not. I'm seeing it anyway. You might see

this kind of stuff all the time, but not me. I'm used to picking up on vibes, you know? Who is about to ask someone out, whose ex is going to show up unannounced. Who should get a checkup at the doctor, that sort of thing. Party tricks compared to this nightmare."

"You should eat. You're so thin," Liz said. She nudged the plate back.

"No one ever tells me that." Jones crammed a fork into a hunk of kale.

"I want to talk to the ones who worked the case back when his mom died. Around the time those other boys disappeared." Liz pulled out her phone, scrolled. "Maybe there's something there."

"Good idea. Hey, I'm sorry, Vi. I never thought of what this might be doing to you."

"Just get the bastard, okay?"

"We'll do our best."

I knew they'd try. I hoped it would be enough.

***

A week later, no new victims. I hoped the trail wouldn't get cold, but more than that I hoped Ida'd been scared off. I knew anything Jade could remember, if she pushed herself, would help. I knew something was coming even if I couldn't say what.

"We need to sit down together, okay?"

"Of course. Liz is running down alibis for the other nights, but later tonight, okay? How's that?"

By the end of the day, we had a plan to meet at Jones' place, including Jade.

"Look, I've got to tell you all something, and I don't want you freaking out." Jones poured some glasses of wine and pulled a club soda out of the fridge for Jade. Liz sank into the sofa.

WHAT HAPPENED WAS IMPOSSIBLE

Liz set a hand on my knee and scooted closer. "What is it?" Her voice was low and smooth. Loving.

Jade shot Jones a sharp glance. Jones shrugged.

"It's getting personal." My voice was too quiet. Afraid.

Jade let out a small gasp.

"I think he's coming after me."

"Whoa, wait a minute. What?" Jones jumped up.

Liz motioned for me to go on.

I let out a deep breath, hands on my knees. "Okay. I think he knows I'm onto him. Like, maybe he's psychic, too."

"No way. No way! I invite a psychic into one investigation, and she ends up a target. Awesome."

"Shit," Jade said. "How do you know?"

"It's like he's watching me watch him. I swear I can feel him. In my head. I know that's totally screwed up. The other day I was thinking about the case, going through the details. Then all of a sudden. Boom!"

Jade knotted up her face, chewing on her lower lip. Tears welled in her eyes.

"It was my face this time. With 'Victim 8' scrawled on the forehead. *My* forehead."

"Shit." Jade had nothing else to say.

"Is it possible that you're wrong? Maybe just getting too close?" Liz asked.

Jade got up and poured herself another club soda. It didn't take a psychic to know she wished it were something stronger. "No way, Liz. Vi's never wrong."

"This is a nightmare. We'll protect you, okay?" Liz squeezed my hand.

Jones squirmed. "I'm glad you two hit it off and all, but let's make sure she's not in danger before the flirting goes any further, okay?"

"No. He hasn't decided on who's next yet. He's distracting you with a threat, you know?" Jade's voice was breathy and fast.

"Is that really possible?"

"Trust me. I know him. You believe Vi's psychic. He can sense it somehow. Why wouldn't he push back?" Jade had a way of asking questions that provoked answers. Damn philosophers.

"You're saying he's psychic?" Jones asked.

"I'm saying he has a talent for—persuasion. I've seen it." Jade moved to the window, pinched the bridge of her nose like her head hurt. "The day our mom died—was *murdered*—I saw him at school. Going into the bathroom."

"So? That proves he wasn't there, Jade." Jones couldn't make the leap, but I was seeing the pieces fall together.

"He had a tube of lipstick in his hand. The shade Mom wore."

"That doesn't mean—what are you saying?"

I went to Jade, waved Jones off. "I'd put good money on it being the same shade you're finding on the victims."

Jones and Liz settled into a tense pause. The room felt electric with anticipation.

"He made her do it." Jade spit out the words like she'd held them inside until they fermented too long.

"Jade—" Jones started.

"I don't know how!" Jade's fingers curled into fists.

"What does that mean for us today?" Jones finally asked. "You're connected because you're related. Can he connect with anyone or only those with certain dispositions? Abilities? Like Violet?"

WHAT HAPPENED WAS IMPOSSIBLE

"Well, how would I know? It's not like I go to Psychics Anonymous. We don't have meetings."

"Right, sorry. Dumb question," Jones said. A flood of pink rose on her cheeks.

"But if he can communicate with you—" Liz started. She didn't finish the thought. She didn't have to.

***

The plan was simple enough.

Get Ida to think we weren't following him anymore. Seed him into a false sense of security. Convince him the cops had another lead, then another suspect. Block him out of my mind for good.

We hoped if we were headed in some other direction, he'd pick up on his obsession again, and hopefully drop his interest in me along the way. The big difference would be that this time, they'd be waiting for him.

"How can you tell if he's listening?" Jade asked.

"How the hell would I know? It's not like being on Zoom," I said.

Jones laughed out loud, and then tacked on a "Sorry."

"This isn't funny," Liz said. She swatted Jones on the shoulder.

"Obviously not. I know that."

"Look, I can try, but I can't make any guarantees. I've never done anything like this." A lot rested on my shoulders. "Walk me through. Tell me what you're going to do."

Jade gnawed on her fingernails. "No way! You can't keep her in the loop anymore," she said.

"What? Of course you can. I need to know what's happening."

"No, she's right," Liz said. "What if he, I don't know, hacks you or something and finds out it's a con? It'll just piss him off."

"I'm not a computer. He can't hack me."

"Look, you just said it's nothing you've done before, so you can't really be sure. What if he's a more powerful psychic than you? What if he can see through the veil? You can't risk getting this psychopath angry, you know? He's dangerous," Jade said. She looked like she was going to throw up.

"So you're highjacking me to lay out a cover story, and I'm just supposed to go along with it?" I flopped onto the couch. "You're supposed to be the sensitive one, Jade, and you're shutting me down, too."

Jade said nothing.

"Damn straight we are. Jade's right. We can't let him catch on," Liz said. "Let's stop talking about it now, in fact. Like an inoculation, we have to create a brick wall in your mind."

"How am I supposed to do that exactly?" My voice quaked.

Liz shrugged. "Pull out all the stops. Noise machines, music, meditation. You're into all that, right?"

"Yeah, sure. I have a wave machine I use to sleep, so I guess . . . "

"What about your dreams?" Jade asked. "Can he get into them?"

"God, I hope not." Jones' face paled.

BAIT

Jade Wright

I MADE MYSELF a promise, and I meant it. I was not going to die. Not tonight. Not because of my sociopathic brother. I wasn't going to let him kill Vi either.

There was a mental game afoot, and I wanted to win. For once. Knock Ida down the way he knocked everyone around us down. That was my angle.

Behind the scenes a terrible trifecta plotting to bring down a serial killer with a psychic on the outside. Jones the eager detective, me the sister and resident philosopher, and Liz the Wiz Kid profiler. All of us blocking a psychic. They wouldn't risk putting a tail on Ida, so they didn't.

But that didn't mean we couldn't frequent his hot spots. Violet told us about a bar she'd seen in her visions a few times, Capers over on Third Street. A lonely-hearts club kind of pickup place for middle-aged folks. Complete with 90's nights and happy hour specials.

I was going to hate it, but that's what I signed on for. He hadn't seen me in years. Not in person or through the mind. That meant safety. In a way. And if he recognized me, he probably wouldn't assume I had anything to do with the case. He was too secure to worry about someone as insignificant as me. It'd just be a chance meeting with an estranged sibling. No harm. I would be spared his suspicion. If anyone could be safe around a serial killer.

Was it a risk stepping into his path? Sure. Did I have a choice? Not much.

"I'm off." I stuffed a book into my bag.

"Reading material? At a bar?" Liz asked.

"What? It's how I roll."

"It's conspicuous. It'll make you look out of place," she said.

I buttoned up my worn peacoat and turned up the collars for emphasis. "I'm a philosophy professor. I always look out of place. Besides, the more uncomfortable I am, the more he's likely to zero in on me, right? Maybe he'll recognize me and want to catch up."

Jones held out her arms like she was stopping a fight. "She's not wrong. She marches to a different drummer, Liz. Drop it."

"Besides, I'm bait. If I'm going to provoke a monster, then I decide what I'm doing in the bar, okay?"

Liz opened her mouth, about to speak.

"The core ethical issue here is consent, okay? And it's mine to grant. I know what I'm getting into. Don't worry about it."

"Thanks for breaking it down for us." Liz said. "You're sure he can't, you know, read you the way he's pushing back on Vi?"

"Sure? No. But I can tell you I've been grayrocking him for as long as I can remember. Like when I could talk, I was shutting him out. Actively. I told you, something always told me he was dangerous and I learned to stay out of his way."

WHAT HAPPENED WAS IMPOSSIBLE

"He can't break through? Reach you?" Jones took a step closer to me.

"I'm not psychically connected that way. Not with anyone. Shit, I can barely sense my own emotions, let alone anyone else's."

Jones laughed. "Fair point."

"Fine. What do I know. I'm only the expert profiler." Liz shook her head. "Jesus, she's a handful, huh?"

"Always." I gave them a thumbs up. "Now, if we're all agreed don't let him kill me or Violet and we're cool. Otherwise, I'm going to spoil my calm, and I don't want to spoil my calm." I attempted a smile.

God knows how, under the circumstances.

Liz's body tightened. "I'm really not sure about this. Wait, you know what? I'm totally sure. This is a crap idea. We should be sending in someone with training. Someone who can handle him if things take a turn."

"He has been to the precinct. If he's half as smart as we think, he's probably memorized the faces of the women on the force."

"All four of them?" Liz interrupted.

"Very funny. We should've been more careful from the gate with him. I don't like putting my friend in this situation, but we aren't swarming with options."

"By the way, I got nothing on him from Murdock and Gutierrez. Unless you count the bad feeling Ida gave them all those years ago."

"Look, you guys are everywhere, we're more than 90% sure he's guilty, and I'm wearing a wire. Catch him before it goes bad, okay?"

One last thing to remember. I'm not going to die tonight.

CRIME SCENE

AT HOME ALONE, Violet screamed. Drenched in sweat, the potent smell of bleach stung her eyes and nostrils. *He was cleaning up a crime scene.* She could smell it.

He saw me. I know he saw me. It was like he was looking at me through a mirror while I watched him.

The woman, begging alone in the dark just before she lost consciousness. Her face streaked with blood and dirt, like she'd been dragged somewhere. Her hands were caked with mud, tied behind her back, fastened to something—a pole? Was she outside? The air was moving on her face, matted hair catching in her mouth. Then a whirring sound.

The hum of a fan?

His eyes like ice. His hands were steady and calm. Nothing bothered him.

Her face. His face. Her face. His face. Over and over again.

The vision stuck like tar, hot and blistering.

What was that place? That sound?

Violet shivered. *It's like I'm the one doing it. I'm killing her.*

Violet knew better than to call. Not tonight. Not at all. Not now. They'd sworn her to secrecy, insisted she be cut out of the investigation since she'd felt his presence. Too bad that didn't make it stop.

Violet sat up in bed and pressed the sheet flat with her hands. She let out a slow, long exhale. The room went cold. Not the room. Her blood.

"Okay. If you won't get out of my head, I'm getting into yours."

***

Violet couldn't catch her breath. She wasn't sure if Ida had sensed her, but she felt his eyes on her. Even at home alone. She peered outside. An unmarked car sat by the construction zone where they were putting in the new condos. Just as Liz promised.

In case.

In case of what?

In case the worst possible thing happened, that's what.

She shivered and glanced at the clock. Midnight. She pulled on a thick robe and went to the kitchen.

"Can't sleep, may as well have some tea." Had she been wrong about Capers? Was Wright playing some kind of trick, messing with her head?

She put the kettle on and sat down in the kitchen, massaging her temple with a thumb. Waiting for the tea, her mind rambled. Water rises to a boil slowly, then it rumbles and hisses. *Brick wall, Violet. Be a brick wall.*

Planning a murder was probably a lot like that, too.

"Jesus, this is fucked up." She thought she heard a click. A door opening?

No. It was in her head.

"Hello stranger," a voice came.

His voice.

"Ready to play a game of chase?"

Dear God, he was taunting her.

Violet paced the floor, sick to her stomach that she'd been wrong about the bar. Something about that sound. The mud.

"Oh shit." She grabbed the phone. "Pick up, pick up, pick up."

***

A few miles away, Jade sat at a bar, bored. By the time she spotted Ida in the back of the room, she moved twice to make sure it was him. Each time, Jade positioned herself further from the crowd, at a more isolated seat than the last.

He was there all right. Prowling for a victim. The sight of her brother made her skin crawl.

Since no one knew how he picked the women, Jade scanned the room, searching for someone who seemed vulnerable. A potential victim. Someone nervous and alone, maybe drunk. But most of the tables were full. A happy crowd.

Their eyes caught. She was sure he saw her. She didn't smile or make an inviting gesture. Too obvious. Too confident. Too unlike the girl he'd erased all those years ago.

He didn't acknowledge her.

That was familiar.

He hadn't been much more welcoming than her dad when she came out. If anything, he encouraged dear old Dad in the other direction.

Ida seemed posed, sitting there. He made eye contact with anyone who noticed him, smiling, nodding, but very alone.

Jade eyed him from a distance, but he didn't sit with anyone, didn't speak. Sipping a beer, taking in the crowd, Wright made no effort to talk to anyone, including Jade.

After spotting him, there was a whole lot of nothing. It went on long enough that Jade started to doubt Violet's insights as much as her own. How precise could a psychic be? How much could anyone rely on childhood fears?

Wright didn't exactly look like a predator on the hunt. At least not tonight. He looked awkward. *Almost as awkward as me.* Wright never made a move. In fact, he didn't approach anyone. Instead, he hovered, like a thing just out of reach. A ghost.

Maybe Ida wasn't the monster of a brother she recalled. The whiny kid she knew was gone. All that sat across the bar from her was an unremarkable man. Still, something about him gave her the creeps. *Maybe tonight just wasn't the night, after all.*

***

"What's up, Violet? You're not supposed to be calling," Jones said.

"He's here. It's me," Violet whispered, her voice hoarse.

"Impossible. We've got eyes on him at Capers, but he's not doing anything."

"I heard him. He's *here.*"

"Here, where?"

"At the apartment. I think he's in the hall. He's still after me."

"Look, Jade's been watching him all night, and besides, you've got eyes outside. Don't you see the car?"

"Don't you get it? That explains the odd numbering. He's more than psychic. He uses people, controls them, gets in their heads. What if the numbers aren't clues?"

"You're not making sense."

"Turn it around. They are just details. Of how they're connected."

"We know that, Vi."

"No. It's more than that. It's how he lines them up. Connects them in a chain. How many it takes to hold them."

"Like captives? With what?"

"Like sigils to him. The numbers are maps. Coordinates. He tracks how many people he's used to set up the scene. They're like his way of recording what happened. They hold everything."

"Vi, you're suggesting he's got help? People following him like some kind of cult leader?"

"No. They don't know they're tied to him. He picks up on minor psychic connections like a radio sending out a constant signal. He uses them. Influences them."

"Is that how he found you?"

"I think so. It's how he stages his alibis. By making people see things that aren't there."

"Wait, what? You're saying he's not at Capers? That's impossible."

"All of it's impossible, isn't it?"

Wright hadn't made a move on Jade or anyone else. But Violet sounded urgent with panic. With certainty.

"You're not listening. He can make people see things, he's got a kind of power. He's a pusher. I saw what's next, not what's past. The next victim will come through the new development in my neighborhood. The mud, the poles—it was the frame of the condos they're building."

"Okay, okay, I'm listening. We'll clear out and head to the site."

WHAT HAPPENED WAS IMPOSSIBLE

"He's coming for me."

"When?"

"Now. The wave machine by my bed. That's what I heard. Not a fan. He's coming here. You have to hurry." Her voice was desperate, pleading.

"I can't say I understand, but we're on our way. We'll send someone to get Jade and radio for backup."

Liz didn't ask what Violet said. She turned the sirens on.

"Forget protocol, we're going," Liz said. She leaned forward, hands on the dashboard.

"She'll be okay. So you believe psychics are a credible source now?"

Liz shook her head. "I believe Violet."

She dialed a number on her cell. No answer. She dialed another.

"Check out the construction zone. Anything unusual, you tell me."

***

At the apartment, Liz and Jones bolted up the stairs. Violet's door was open. They went in without a word, guns drawn. A murmur of voices echoed at the end of the hall. Violet's bedroom.

Liz took the lead.

Wright had his back to the door. His hands clutched Violet by the throat, pressing her into a corner. Terror in her eyes, she didn't look up. A messy, bright red "8" was already lipsticked onto her forehead. His fingers crimson from smearing it.

Wright wouldn't let himself get caught like this.

He pressed a knife along Violet's cheek, but didn't slice.

Wright didn't turn around. Too focused. Too confident.

"Get away from her," Liz said. Planted in the doorway, she had a perfect shot. She didn't take it.

Wright clenched his fingers around Violet's throat again and she squirmed, choking. "You worthless—"

"I know you're not about to call my friend a bitch."

"One move, that's all it'd take, Wright. Give me a reason." Liz aimed. "Let her go."

After a beat, he released his grip. Violet collapsed into a heap.

"I'm going to count backwards from one thousand." Ida turned, faced the police, grinning. "Then you'll let me go."

MEDIA MAN

Detective Jones

IDA **WRIGHT IN** custody was a strange phenomenon. He adored the attention, the blitz. Once the reporters got him talking, there was only one subject: himself. His horrifying past. Ordeals at school. Problems with family. The teachers who adored him but taught him nothing. The self-made man he became after a world of tragedies dumped on his shoulders.

Even a few folks on the department found him endearing. I guess it was hard not to root for a guy who seemed to have so much going against him. The echo chamber of popular opinion had its own kind of momentum.

"It was hard to find a girl who really listened, someone who cared what you thought and felt. Whatever that woman said about me, she's invented half of it. I'll tell you that."

"I thought we had an arrangement."

Reporters scribbled down his comments, reposted them nonstop.

Ida smiled for selfies, posed as people snapped pictures of him on the street.

They had to pin it on someone, and I'm the nearest thing they have to a suspect. How messed up is that?

Angry face. Thumbs up.

Violet knows nothing about me. We had one messed up encounter. She twisted it into something it wasn't. Check her phone.

I'm not opening those comments.

When it comes to love, I'll keep looking.

Heart eyes.

For a murderer.

She's out there. Waiting for me. I'll find her.

My stomach churned at the thought, but I refrained from adding a puke-face emoji to his thread.

Where's she now, anyway? Hiding? She should hide. She should be embarrassed to show her face after what she invited me to do. Without even meeting her first. Online dating, amirite?

And that's misogyny bingo! It didn't take him too long to get to the slut shaming. Poor Vi. Sure the department found a series of messages on an app between Vi and an unknown number, but she swore she hadn't seen them before. I believed her but that didn't count for much.

Laughing emojis, wow emojis, likes. *Unbelievable.*

I'm being criticized for my offbeat choices, but I work harder than anyone I know. Everyone deserves the benefit of the doubt, don't they?

Thumbs up, smiley face, heart.

A little thing called presumed innocence.

Heart, heart, heart.

What bullshit.

***

Ida Wright never confessed. Not really. Instead he organized his thoughts into an escape ladder, something to use at any opportunity. A statement for the deposition. Bite-sized one-liners for interviews. A manifesto. Every phrase as memorable as it was rehearsed. Ida Wright had a brand. His was the familiar narrative of the falsely accused.

He was built for attention like this. Before long, he wanted more of it. And he got it. News sources and bloggers, whether he requested interviews or they did, the mechanisms behind the scenes worked in his favor. Feigned sincerity transferred well. He worked the angles until his side of events was heard before the courts had a chance at him. Damn the evidence.

"People love tragedies, don't they? Women do, anyway. I'm like a fixer-upper, a real rom-com hero type. Rude or rough on the outside but full of wonders. That's practically my biography. I've had it hard my whole life and now the cops are determined to blame me for things I didn't do just to wrap up the case."

The police chief made a public statement about persuasive evidence and open minds, but nobody tuned in. Too factual, too boring. Even copaganda couldn't withstand Ida's ego.

HIS ONLY DAGGER WAS STABBING LONELINESS:
WRIGHT SPEAKS OUT ABOUT . . . LOVE?

Exclusive Interview with Accused Killer

PEOPLE LINED UP to vouch for Ida Wright. Monica Sedgewick. Old teachers. Neighbors. Business partners. The news ran hot with testaments to his character. Everyone but his sister Jade. She stayed as far away as she could get. No one would've believed what she suspected. No one would've even listened. She wasn't credible.

As intended, Ida's last interview with *The Independent Voice* drew clicks.

IV: What can you tell readers about yourself that they haven't seen on the news?

IW: The news? Oh, that's all one-sided, isn't it? I guess everybody loves a backstory, don't they? Especially women.

IV: Why do you say that?

WHAT HAPPENED WAS IMPOSSIBLE

IW: You don't believe me? Watch a romance. So many of them hinge on a sweet confessional moment when a dude spills his tragedies like wine. It's a crackpot setup, but romance feeds on that mess. Wine makes a pretty bad stain, though, and once it sets, there's no way to get it out.

IV: And what do you think that has to do with you?

IW: Well it's a really simple story. Only a true love, soulmate, or best match can knit together the holes in a broken man's heart. That's what I want, too. See, you're a broken man, like me, a guy who's been hurt a lot, you learn to figure out which women are prepared to do that kind of patchwork.

IV: So you want to talk about love?

IW: I know it's not glamorous, but I wanted to find someone. Someone to believe in me and make all my imperfections okay. I learned to let pain fill in the gaps so I seemed deep and sincere, longing. What happened with that woman—that Violet— was a misunderstanding. I wasn't going to hurt her. I thought she was as interested as I was.

IV: And you think people can relate to that part of your story?

IW: You're probably judging me a little, but I'm not ashamed to admit my childhood tragedies might have attracted the wrong kind of people into my life. My pain defined me, you know? Wounds. Dark. Deep. Impossible to remove. The best thing to do was cover them up because some messes just wouldn't clean.

IV: And Violet was the wrong kind of woman?

IW: Don't try to trip me up. I'm not talking about her character. I'm saying I have certain inclinations (smiles). My love life depended on women who saw all of me, the kind that enjoyed sadness in a guy. The ones unafraid to swim into it. They lap up heartache like piranhas scenting blood. But sometimes that swirl of tragedy could be a whirlpool that tugged them right down, deep into the bottom of a place they didn't want to see unless they could really handle me.

IV: Vi is one of the ones who couldn't handle you?

IW: Yes. That's it. She changed her mind or something. Like a he-said-she-said situation. With all these other things going on, I became a convenient—what's the word—scapegoat.

IV: Sounds like a trap.

IW: (nods). I'm not that clever, you know? I was just looking for a fun time. A little roleplaying.

IV: And Violet—

IW: (laughs). I couldn't have seen that trap coming. Because people— women, I mean, they usually believed me. They wanted to believe in me. But Violet was out to get me from the start. I wasn't surprised to find out she was working with the cops. Were you?

IV: Sorry, I'm here to ask you the questions. I don't want to comment on that.

WHAT HAPPENED WAS IMPOSSIBLE

IW: Right, of course.

IV: Do you think talking like this, opening up to our readers, might help set you free?

IW: Well sure! Yes. I believe in this country. I believe the average person wants to do the right thing. Fighting for an underdog like me is a good cause. I know people will pick up my story. Talk about me. Advocate for my innocence.

IV: Sounds like an attention goldmine.

IW: Opportunities like this interview can make a real difference in a high-profile case. Knowing the town is behind me can move a mountain.

IV: So what else do you have to share with our readers? Anything personal?

IW: (laughs). Like what kind of woman I'm looking for?

IV: If you like. How do you figure it out?

IW: Sure, Sure. I can talk about that. I know right away. Like on a first meeting.

IV: Love at first sight?

IW: Sort of. I mean, I'm honest about who I am. My past. My problems. I drop some heavy hints about my annoying habits and kinks, but I tell them right away it's just quirky, you know? Coping mechanisms. It's painful, being honest, but it's better to know. For both of us.

IV: Do you talk about being interviewed by the police?

IW: I haven't been out on a date since this mess started.

IV: I mean, the other times.

IW: No. I mean, you can't lay it all out on the first night. If they aren't getting me, I'll explain. My past was brutal, but women cherish honesty, you know?

IV: All women?

IW: No. I'm not generalizing. Responses usually go in a few ways: courteous but concerned, intrigued and curious, or disinterested.

IV: Say more about that.

IW: Courteous women stay polite. They don't press the point, but I can tell they care. That's okay, but I won't ask disinterested women out twice. Why bother? They don't see me.

IV: So you don't want to string them on.

IW: Right. I shouldn't have to try that hard with everything I've been through. The ones that can't resist the hinted pain are the ones I want. Maybe the daggers in my soul are an aphrodisiac. All I need is someone who isn't afraid to see them. When I give up the truth, some women can't resist me. I thought Violet was one of those women. The kind who adore men who've been through pain. She wasn't. But the ones who do, those are the gals who will see this sham for what it is. They're railroading me.

WHAT HAPPENED WAS IMPOSSIBLE

IV: Who? Women?

IW: Very funny. No, not women. I love women. The police force. They're framing me.

IV: Why would they do that?"

IW: I don't know. For a quick resolution, I guess.

IV: And why you?

IW: Look, I've had so many things go wrong. I guess I just look like an easy target.

IV: What's gone wrong, Ida? Can you share it for those who haven't read about your background?

IW: Well, first my dad's suicide. Then my mother's. Can you imagine? Then the strange crimes in my hometown.

IV: When was this?

IW: When I was a teenager. In high school. A few boys went missing. I knew some of them.

IV: And were you a suspect?

IW: (shakes head). No way. Never. Ask anyone on the case.

IV: I'm sure someone has.

IW: And if so, there's the proof. They were digging into my past, trying to turn me into a suspect.

IV: Anything else?

IW: (nods). Once Robert—my dad—died, I'd had the end of it. I sold his place, fast as I could with a realtor I worked with over the years. Now it's missing women in the same town. Women I didn't know. Women I had nothing to do with. See? All I did was sell a piece of real estate, and my name got mixed into the mess because of my past here. It's ridiculous.

IV: Do you think anyone out there empathizes with you?

IW: What do you mean?

IV: Do you think someone will advocate for you? Care about your pain, your loss as much as you?

IW: Sure. Yes. That's why I'm doing this interview. That and to put it out there.

IV: Put what out there?

IW: (laughs). My relationship status, I guess. Just be real. I want to find someone, you know? Who would go out with a guy accused of all this? (looks away). I've got to make my own case, I guess.

IV: This isn't a dating profile, Ida. It's an interview.

IW: Right, I know, but still. No one but me will set the record straight.

IV: Okay then. Anything you want to add?

IW: Let me be specific about Violet. That's the only person I'm connected to because the police literally barged in on a date. I had no way of knowing it was a trap. Actual entrapment. I thought she was the kind of woman who would understand me. She had baggage too, you know?

WHAT HAPPENED WAS IMPOSSIBLE

Then it turns out she's dating a woman on the case, and friends with my freak of a sister. I mean, I think that's all a little too suspicious. Not to stereotype, but that's a lot of man-hater-bonding. I'm just the final guy they've decided to blame in their desperate search to pin this on someone. And the police department had the power to put together the pieces.

IV: That's pretty strong stuff.

IW: (shrugs). I was just looking for a date. Someone who could stand all that pain, someone who could absorb it. Carry it with me. I wanted love. Who doesn't? I deserved it like anyone else. I guess I'll keep looking until I find her.

IV: I know this is off task, but what do you think she'll be like? This dream woman of yours. Do you know?

IW: Oh, I know all right. Someone who believes in me. Someone exactly like Mom.

ABOUT THE AUTHOR

E. F. Schraeder is the author of the Imadjinn Award finalist *Liar: Memoir of a Haunting* (Omnium Gatherum, 2021), *As Fast as She Can* (Sirens Call Publications, 2022), a story collection, and several poetry chapbooks. Schraeder's first full-length poetry collection, *The Price of a Small Hot Fire,* is forthcoming from Raw Dog Screaming Press. Part time librarian and full-time horror fan, Schraeder is also a hot pepper enthusiast who believes in ghosts, magic, and dogs.

SPOOKY TALES FROM GHOULISH BOOKS 2023

LIKE REAL | Shelly Lyons
ISBN: 978-1-943720-82-8 $16.95
This mind-bending body horror rom-com is a rollicking Cronenbergian gene splice of *Idle Hands* and *How to Lose a Guy in 10 Days*. It's freaky. It's fun. It's LIKE REAL.

XCRMNTMNTN | Andrew Hilbert
ISBN: 978-1-943720-81-1 $14.95
When a pile of shit from space lands near a renowned filmmaker's set, inspiration strikes. Take a journey up a cosmic mountain of excrement with the director and his film crew as they ascend into madness led only by their own vanity and obsession. This is a nightmare about creation. This is a dream about poop. This is a call to arms against vowels. This is *XCRMNTMNTN*.

BOUND IN FLESH | edited by Lor Gislason
ISBN: 978-1-943720-83-5 $16.95
Bound in Flesh: An Anthology of Trans Body Horror brings together 13 trans and non-binary writers, using horror to both explore the darkest depths of the genre and the boundaries of flesh. A disgusting good time for all! Featuring stories by Hailey Piper, Joe Koch, Bitter Karella, and others.

CONJURING THE WITCH | Jessica Leonard
ISBN: 978-1-943720-84-2 $16.95
Conjuring the Witch is a dark, haunted story about what those in power are willing to do to stay in power, and the sins we convince ourselves are forgivable.

WHAT HAPPENED WAS IMPOSSIBLE |
E. F. Schraeder
ISBN: 978-1-943720-85-9 $14.95
Everyone knows the woman who escapes a massacre is a final girl, but who is the final boy? *What Happened Was Impossible* follows the life of Ida Wright, a man who knows how to capitalize on his childhood tragedies . . . even when he caused them.

THE ONLY SAFE PLACE LEFT IS THE DARK|
Warren Wagner

ISBN: 978-1-943720-86-6 $14.95

In *The Only Safe Place Left is the Dark*, an HIV positive gay man must leave the relative safety of his cabin in the woods to brave the zombie apocalypse and find the medication he needs to stay alive.

THE SCREAMING CHILD| Scott Adlerberg

ISBN: 978-1-943720-87-3 $16.95

Scott Adlerberg's *The Screaming Child* is a mystery horror novel told by a grieving woman working on a book about an explorer who was murdered in a remote wilderness region, only to get caught up in a dangerous journey after hearing the distant screams from her own vanished child somewhere in the woods.

RAINBOW FILTH | Tim Meyer

ISBN: 978-1-943720-88-0 $14.95

Rainbow Filth is a weirdo horror novella about a small cult that believes a rare psychedelic substance can physically transport them to another universe.

LET THE WOODS KEEP OUR BODIES| E. M. Roy

ISBN: 978-1-943720-89-7 $16.95

The familiar becomes strange the longer you look at it. Leo Bates navigates a broken sense of reality, shattered memories, and a distrust of herself in order to find her girlfriend Tate and restore balance to their hometown of Eston—if such a thing ever existed to begin with.

SAINT GRIT| Kayli Scholz

ISBN: 978-1-943720-90-3 $14.95

One brooding summer, Nadine Boone pricks herself on a poisonous manchineel tree in the Florida backcountry. Upon self-orgasm, Nadine conjures a witch that she calls Saint Grit. Pitched as *Gummo* meets *The Craft*, Saint Grit grows inside of Nadine over three decades, wreaking repulsive havoc on a suspicious cast of characters in a small town known as Sugar Bends. Comes in Censored or Uncensored cover.

Ghoulish Books
PO Box 1104
Cibolo, TX 78108

☐ LIKE REAL	16.95
☐ XCRMNTMNTN	14.95
☐ BOUND IN FLESH	16.95
☐ CONJURING THE WITCH	16.95
☐ WHAT HAPPENED WAS IMPOSSIBLE	14.95
☐ THE ONLY SAFE PLACE LEFT IS THE DARK	14.95
☐ THE SCREAMING CHILD	16.95
☐ RAINBOW FILTH	14.95
☐ LET THE WOODS KEEP OUR BODIES	16.95
☐ SAINT GRIT	14.95
Censored | Uncensored	

Ship to:

Name _____

Address _____

City_____State_____Zip _____

Phone Number _____

Book Total: $_____

Shipping Total: $_____

Grand Total: $_____

Not all titles available for immediate shipping. All credit card purchases must be made online at GhoulishBooks.com. Shipping is 5.80 for one book and an additional dollar for each additional book. Contact us for international shipping prices. All checks and money orders should be made payable to Perpetual Motion Machine.

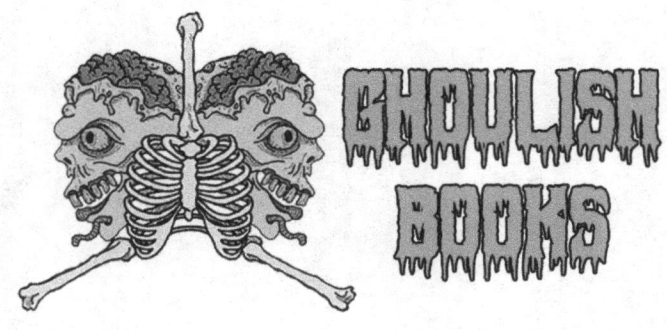

Patreon:
www.patreon.com/pmmpublishing

Website:
www.GhoulishBooks.com

Facebook:
www.facebook.com/GhoulishBooks

Twitter:
@GhoulishBooks

Instagram:
@GhoulishBookstore

Newsletter:
www.PMMPNews.com

Linktree:
linktr.ee/ghoulishbooks

Patreon:

www.ingramcontent.com/pod-product-compliance
Lightning Source LLC
Chambersburg PA
CBHW011518240626
47154CB00010B/3081